FOR THE WIN

Amber Garza

To Kagen, for proving that dreams really do come true.

PART 1
BEFORE

CHAPTER 1
London

I wasn't expecting to like him.

Not one bit.

I had known guys like Cooper Montgomery before. Egotistical jocks who thought they owned the world and everything in it. And not once had they treated me with any ounce of respect. I was the shy girl. The one with her nose always pressed in a book. I certainly wasn't the popular or the pretty girl. As a society, we'd been conditioned from childhood about what was cool and what wasn't. The message had always been clear. Intelligent, bookish girls were not sexy. Lucky for me, I had never wanted to be sexy. Quite the opposite, in fact.

All I'd ever wanted was to blend in. To fade into the background where no one would bother me at all. I wanted to be left alone, plain and simple. I'd learned the hard way what it was like to garner attention, and that was something I never wanted to experience again.

That's why guys like Cooper were an enigma to me. I didn't understand people who welcomed the spotlight, and craved the attention. Even though I'd never spoken to Cooper, I'd seen him around school. He always had a group surrounding him, as if he was afraid to be alone. Girls trailed him like he was their god or something. Frankly, I found it repulsive. And

I had no desire to be any part of it.

It's the reason I was so upset when I was told by John, the editor of the school newspaper, that I had to interview him. I was all set to write my hard-hitting piece on the lack of nutritional choices available in our cafeteria. But instead I'd been assigned a sports piece, and I knew literally nothing about sports. The only reason we were even doing this article on Cooper was because Annabelle Garcia had a huge crush on him. She'd pitched the idea at our last brainstorming session, and then immediately offered to write the story. I was a little surprised because I hadn't even realized our school had a fall ball season. Apparently Annabelle knew more about baseball than me. Too bad she was out this week with the flu.

I begged John to push back the story, but he said that Cooper was expecting to be interviewed this afternoon. And that's how I found myself trekking across campus toward the baseball field after school. As I neared the ball field, I noticed the curious glances from the players. I knew I didn't look at all like a normal spectator. For starters, my jeans and long-sleeved shirt were not conducive to the California fall heat. But I'd always been conservative in my attire. My dad and my friend, Skyler, were the only people who understood my need to stay covered up. The difference was that Skyler was always trying to get me to loosen up, while I was pretty sure my dad was hoping I'd remain this way forever.

Clutching the pad of paper tightly to my chest, I stepped onto the grass. My tennis shoes sank into it with every step. The warm sun beat down on my back, and sweat gathered along my shoulder blades and spine. I longed for cooler fall temperatures, but we never really had a fall. It didn't start cooling down until November most years, and it was only September now. Therefore, I needed to remain patient. Even when we were blessed with rain the other day, the air was still sticky and warm. I blew the bangs off my forehead and walked over to the bleachers. They were empty, so I took a seat in the first row, setting my pad of paper and pen down on my lap.

Cooper stood on the mound wearing his orange and black Gold Rush High School Tigers' hat, along with a shirt bearing the emblem of our school, and white pants. He adjusted the ball cap on his head before bringing his arm back for the pitch. When the ball left his hand, it moved so fast it was difficult to see where it went. The batter missed, and it was called a strike. Despite myself, I was impressed.

I'd heard Cooper was good, but I'd never witnessed it. Attending baseball games was not my idea of fun. In fact, when I was younger my dad used to drag me out to professional baseball games, but I never actually watched them. Instead I'd bring my current book and read until the game ended. I finished many good novels that way. I was pretty sure Dad had been hoping I would gain an appreciation for baseball by going with him to the games, but all I did was gain a sunburn. Eventually he stopped taking me, and I was grateful.

Since I knew zilch about baseball, I decided

to come early to watch some of the practice. This may not have been the story I was hoping for, but I would still write a damn good piece. I was nothing if not professional. No matter the assignment, I made sure I gave it my best. Even when I had to write an article about the cheerleading squad I bit back my scathing remarks and made it as unbiased as I could. Sure John had to modify some of it, but in my defense, the cheerleaders had never made life easy for me. It was difficult to be completely impartial.

However, I had made myself a promise to keep an open mind with this story. And it should've been easy enough, since the article would be about the baseball team and Cooper's position as pitcher. It had nothing to do with his less-than-stellar reputation. Well, less than stellar in my opinion. The rest of the girls at this school seemed to be turned on by his womanizer status.

I watched Cooper strike out a couple more batters before the coach signaled the end of practice. My pulse quickened as the team huddled around the coach, my usual pre-interview jitters hitting me. I wiped my clammy palms on the thigh of my jeans and scanned the questions I'd prepared. My finger moved swiftly over the pad of paper at the questions I'd scrawled in my telltale slanted cursive. My dad always teased me about my penmanship, which he called illegible. But it didn't matter. No one used free hand anymore. Everything was typed on computers. And typing was something I was good at. One day when I was a professional writer I'd lug a laptop with me everywhere. Dad promised to buy me one for Christmas this year, and I was counting down the days. I only hoped he kept his promise. Money was pretty tight for us, but he assured me he was saving up. Usually I stayed cautiously optimistic so I didn't get too upset when it didn't pan out. But this time my heart had already jumped in with both feet before I could catch it and reel it in.

"Hey."

I jolted at the sound of Cooper's voice, not having heard him walk up. My pen rolled off my lap and landed near my feet. Then to my horror, it kept rolling until it landed in the grass.

"I'll grab it," Cooper offered, bending down. When he stood back up, he held the pen out to me. It dangled between his thick fingers.

"Thank you," I mumbled, snatching it from him. The players had dispersed, some of them hiking across the field, bags slung over their shoulders.

"I'm assuming you're the person interviewing me for the paper." Cooper flashed me a smile, a dimple forming on his right cheek.

My heart twisted. I could see why girls found him attractive. Even though I wasn't attracted to him at all, he wasn't exactly ugly.

"Yeah." I stuck out my right hand, while fisting the pen in my left. "London Miller, reporter for the Gold Rush Gazette." *Dear god, I sounded like an idiot.* Why was this guy making me so nervous?

"Cooper Montgomery, but I'm guessing you already knew that." As he shook my hand, he grinned again. His blue eyes sparkled as the sun struck them. I wished I didn't notice how good-looking he was, how perfect his smile was, and how his eyes were bluer than the ocean. But these things were impossible to miss. In the past, I'd only seen Cooper from a distance. This was the closest I'd ever gotten to him, and it seemed he was even better looking close up. I forced away the thoughts, wondering why I allowed my mind to go there in the first place. I wasn't exactly the kind of girl who crushed on guys. I found it pointless, a waste of time and energy. All I wanted in life was to survive high school, and then get into a good college so I could become a reporter. Boys only complicated things. Besides, it's not like any boy was ever interested in me.

"Nice to meet you, London." For some reason hearing my name coming from his lips stopped me cold. A shiver ran down my spine as I drew my hand back.

But I recovered quickly. "Where do you want to conduct the interview?"

"Right here is fine."

"See ya, Coop," one of the players called as he walked past us.

Cooper waved at him before plunking down on the bleacher next to me, so close his thigh brushed mine momentarily.

Swallowing hard, I scooted over a little, putting some space between us. "Great." Biting my lip, I stared down at the pad of paper in my lap. My eyes scanned the paper, searching for a good ice-breaker question. But suddenly they all sounded lame to me. Sighing, I turned to him. "You did great today in practice. I was really impressed."

There was that million dollar smile again. God, this guy was charming. "Thanks. I'm glad to know I impressed you." He threw me a wink.

My cheeks warmed, and I lowered my gaze. Maybe a compliment wasn't the best way to start with this guy. According to John, it's always best to start by buttering the interviewee up. But I had a feeling that Cooper was used to people gushing over him. All I'd succeeded in doing was blowing up his already big head.

"How long have you been playing baseball?" I asked, knowing this would be an easy place to start.

"My whole life." Staring out over the field, a wistful smile flickered. "My mom used to joke that I came out of the womb with a baseball in my hand." An apologetic expression cloaked his face. "Okay, maybe that wasn't that best visual, but you get the point. I was born to play the game."

His answer propelled me forward. I was grateful that he was taking the interview seriously. I'd heard horror stories of football players joking all through their interviews. Even when I did the article on the cheerleaders they weren't all cooperative. Some were sarcastic and giggly. "Did you always know you wanted to pitch?"

"No, actually. When I was a kid I liked to hit." He shrugged, displaying a lopsided grin. *Did he do that just to show off his cute dimple?* I imagined girls became a puddle at his feet when he did that. Luckily, I was stronger than them. "But who doesn't, right?" He paused as if awaiting my response.

Not knowing a thing about baseball, it took me a minute to slowly nod. "Right." I hoped he didn't detect how unenthusiastic I was.

"But when I was around ten, I had a coach who noticed I had a strong arm. He had been a pitcher back when he played, so he kind of took me under his wing; started working with me on pitching. By the end of that season it was clear that I was meant to be a pitcher."

I nodded, giving myself a minute to formulate my next question. My list was invalid at this point. I wanted to keep the momentum of this line of questioning. "What kind of training have you had to get where you are now?"

"I've taken pitching lessons since I was eleven. That was also the year I started playing ball year round. And I practice every spare moment I get."

His words made me wonder if I'd misjudged him. Clearly baseball was his first priority. Before today, I'd always assumed he played ball just to get chicks and hang out with friends. That's the way it appeared from the outside anyway. I thought about the hours I spent immersed in my books and magazines, about all the time I spent writing my articles and stories. Maybe Cooper and I had more in common than I thought.

"Hey, Cooper," a female voice floated in our direction.

I glanced over my shoulder to where a group of girls stood near the fence, smiling. They giggled, flipping their hair around as they waved at Cooper. One of them wore a ball cap on backwards, her blond curls spilling out of it. I recognized most of them. They were the popular girls, the ones who never gave me the time of day. My stomach soured as Cooper waved back, his dimpled smile deepening.

Okay, so maybe I was wrong about him. Clearly we were nothing alike.

CHAPTER 2
Cooper

It was impossible to miss her.

We all noticed her as she stumbled across the field, clutching that damn pad of paper to her chest as if she was terrified of being separated from it. She had to have been roasting in that long-sleeved shirt and jeans. The truth was that we always noticed the girls who came out to watch us practice, but for completely different reasons. Usually we noticed them for their lack of clothing, for their sexy bodies, for the seductive smiles they threw us. The collective raised eyebrows around the team betrayed that the other guys were wondering what the hell this girl was doing out here.

But I knew. I was certain she was the girl interviewing me for that damn article in the school paper. Coach had to force me to do it. To me it seemed like a waste of time. Who read the school paper anyway? I knew I'd never read it. But when Coach insisted that I do something, I did it. Besides, when I mentioned it to my grandparents they were excited. I was pretty sure it would be tacked to the fridge the day I gave it to them, displayed proudly.

While I threw, I could feel her eyes on me. A couple of times I glanced over to see her staring at me intently. I was used to girls watching me, but this felt different. It wasn't in a flirty way. No, she was studying me as if I was a math problem and she had a test tomorrow. I knew I'd seen her around school, but I couldn't remember her name. I think it was a place - like a state or city or something. *Paris? No. Dakota? No, that wasn't it.* Damn it, I couldn't remember.

After practice ended, I headed over to the girl. She sat in the bleachers appearing lost in her own thoughts. When I said hey, she practically jumped out of her skin. Her already large brown eyes widened even more, her pink lips pursing. She was prettier than I imagined. I'd never really looked at her before. She was one of those girls that was easy to bypass, always hidden behind her books and baggy clothes.

When she introduced herself as London, I mentally kicked myself. Of course. *London.* How could I forget a name like that? She clearly wasn't a Paris or a Dakota, but London seemed to fit her. It was obvious that she was nervous when I sat next to her, and I thought it was pretty cute. Sure, girls were always nervous around me, but it usually manifested itself into fits of giggles and twiddling of hair. Nerves made London more determined.

And actually the interview wasn't as painful as I thought it would be. So far she'd stuck to the topic of baseball, and that's how I liked it.

"Hey, Cooper." My head swung upward at the sound of Calista's voice. My skin crawled when I saw her standing with a group of her friends wearing my hat. Shaking my head, I regretted hooking up with her. And what had possessed me to let her borrow my hat? Well, that answer was simple. She

11

looked damn sexy in it when she was wearing next to nothing else, and in that moment I would've said yes to anything. But now she kept acting like she was my girlfriend. Don't get me wrong, she was easy and super hot, but I wasn't interested in having a girlfriend. Falling in love wasn't an option for me. Neither were relationships. I'd already given Calista all I was capable of giving anyone. So why couldn't that be enough?

I groaned inwardly when she sashayed in my direction. As I glanced at London, I couldn't help but notice how irritated she appeared. My ego cropped up and I assumed it was because she was jealous. But as I watched her eyes narrow at Calista, I suspected it had more to do with her than with me. I was sure London wasn't welcome with Calista and her group. In fact, I was ashamed to admit this, but I had no idea who London hung out with.

"Like my hat?" Calista purred, touching my arm.

"Well, it *is* mine," I teased. "So I think you know I like it."

She giggled. "I know, silly. But do you like it on me?"

"You know I do." I smiled, not wishing to be a jerk. I was going to have to have a tough talk with her, but not here. Not in front of a reporter for the school paper and a group of Calista's friends.

Calista's eyes flicked over to London, and she curled her nose. "What's *she* doing here? Is she like your tutor or something?"

London lowered her gaze, fidgeting with her pad of paper. Calista knew I didn't need a tutor. I got

12

straight A's. She was just trying to get under London's skin. And for some reason that irritated me. What had London ever done to her?

"She's interviewing me for the paper," I said, reaching up and adjusting the bill of my cap.

"Oh." A relieved smile spread across her face. Had she been worried when she saw me with London? Surely she didn't think anything was going on between the two of us. London seemed like a nice girl, but she was not my type at all. "Well, I better leave you to it." She leaned over and pecked me on the cheek. "Call me later."

"Okay." I nodded as she scurried back over to her friends.

"Girlfriend?" London asked once the girls had taken off.

"No." I shook my head. "Just a friend."

She raised her eyebrows. "You always kiss your friends?"

"I didn't kiss her, she kissed me. Not that it's any of your business."

This seemed to sober her. She sat up straight. "Right. Sorry. Let's just finish up this interview." Gone was the friendly girl from earlier. This one was all business.

I wondered about her shift in behavior. Had seeing me with Calista really bothered her that much? And if so, why?

"You mentioned that you practice every spare moment you get. What are some ways you practice from home?" She pinned me with a stare.

"I run sometimes in the evenings. And I have a pitching net in my backyard that I throw into."

13

After scribbling something quickly on her paper, she bit her lip. A few strands of dark blond hair slipped over her shoulder as she scanned her notepad wearing a pensive look. None of the girls I dated ever acted this serious. A few more seconds of silence and then her head bobbed up. "You said that your mom jokes about how you were born playing baseball. Would you say that your parents always encouraged your love of the game?"

I nodded, the familiar sick feeling sinking into the pit of my stomach.

She smiled. "That's awesome. I bet they're really proud of you."

"Yeah," I forced the word out, feeling like I might hurl. By the look on her face, I could tell she was going to continue asking more questions about my family. So I hurried to change the subject. "Do you know much about baseball, London?"

Her head snapped up in surprise. "Truthfully, no." Pink spots emerged on her cheeks.

"Come out to the game this Saturday. It's right here at ten a.m."

"What?"

Her flustered behavior made me chuckle. "So you can learn about the game," I explained. "I think it would help with your article."

"Oh. Right. The article. Of course." With a shaky hand, she tucked an errant strand of hair behind her ear revealing a tiny stud that glistened in the sunlight. It looked like the kind of earring a little girl would wear. Not the large hoops or dangly ones like Calista wore. I only recalled that because I kept getting my fingers caught in her damn earrings the other night as we made out.

Had London thought I was inviting her for a different reason? This girl was so hard to read. One minute she acted like she couldn't get away from me fast enough, and the next minute she seemed to want my attention. "And if you have more questions after the game, I'll be happy to answer them."

"Okay. That sounds good." She picked up her notepad and pressed it to her chest. "I guess I've got all I need for now then." Standing up, her lips curled slightly at the edges. "See you Saturday."

"See you then." I tipped my hat.

She whirled around, her shirt floating around her body.

"London?" I called after her.

Craning her neck, she peered at me. A gentle breeze blew kicking up her hair, and it swirled around her face. "Yeah?"

"You might want to wear something different on Saturday."

She narrowed her eyes. "What does that mean?"

"It's just that it's supposed to be in the hundreds, and the games can go for hours. You'll never make it dressed like that."

She shook her head. "Thanks for the heads up, but I think I'm old enough to dress myself." As she stalked off I wondered why my statement offended her so much. That chick was confusing. Now I knew why I stuck to girls like Calista. I liked knowing exactly what I was getting.

CHAPTER 3
London

I pedaled faster as I neared my street. Steering the
bike handle, I turned the corner. Wind whipped in
my face as I passed an apartment complex. Kids
played outside, and their chatter and laughter carried
lightly on the breeze. A car passed, its tires rumbling
on the asphalt. I maneuvered up onto the sidewalk
and my backpack jostled against my spine. The straps
cut into the skin on my shoulders as the wheels spun
beneath me, rolling over the bumps on the concrete.

Even though I was seventeen and had my
license, my main mode of transportation was still my
bike. We only had one vehicle, and Dad needed it for
work. Dad didn't want me to get a job during the
school year because he was afraid it would distract
me from my school work. So I planned to work this
summer to save for a car.

Shifting slightly, I continued to pedal until I
reached the duplex I lived in with my dad. Pulling to
the left, I glided into our driveway. As I hopped off
my bike, I caught sight of Skyler peeking out of her
front window. Skyler's family shared the duplex
adjoined to ours. We'd lived next door to each other
since Dad and I moved to Folsom when I was five.
Propping my bike up on the kickstand, I found
myself hoping that she would stay inside. As I started
to fantasize about curling up on the couch with my

latest novel, Skyler's front door popped open and she stepped out. It's not that I didn't like spending time with Skyler. She was pretty much my only friend, and I enjoyed her company. But I was a loner by nature. I preferred to spend time with my books, living in fictional worlds

Skyler's thick black hair was coiled into a bun on top of her head, and she wore gym shorts and a t-shirt. With her long tanned legs, she walked toward me in her bare feet. Sweat clinging to every inch of my skin, I envied her outfit.

Picking my hair up off my damp neck, I smiled at Skyler. "Hey."

"Hey. How did it go with Cooper?" Skyler raised a brow.

"Fine." I moved around her toward the garage. After unlocking the door, I shoved it open. It rattled on the hinges loudly. Once it was all the way up, I grabbed my bike and wheeled it inside. The scent of musty boxes and dust filled my nostrils.

"That's it? Just fine?" She followed me just like I knew she would.

"Yep." After setting my bike near the wall, I closed and locked the garage door. Darkness enveloped us, so I hurried to the door leading inside the house. After opening it, I flicked on the wall switch and a triangle of light appeared. Trailing me, Skyler's feet slapped on the pavement. Cool air circled me when I stepped into the kitchen. The scent of chicken and spices wafted from the crockpot sitting on the counter. Shrugging my backpack off, I dropped it on the ground and shoved it against the wall with the toe of my shoe.

"C'mon, London. It had to be more than just fine." Skyler crossed her arms over her chest.

Sighing, I made my way over to the crockpot that I had filled with chicken, vegetables and salsa this morning before school. Lifting the lid, steam smacked me in the face. As I tested out the chicken with a fork, Skyler came to stand next to me.

"Stop holding out on me. I want to hear all about it." She leaned her back against the counter and stared at me expectantly.

Placing the lid back on the crockpot, I looked up at her. "There's nothing really to tell. I interviewed him about baseball. He answered my questions. End of story."

"What was he like?" Her eyes sparkled under the kitchen lights.

I frowned, thinking of how he'd acted with Calista. God, I couldn't stand her and her 'mean girls' group. "Just about like you'd expect." However, even as the words left my mouth they felt like lies. It wasn't exactly like I'd expected. In fact, until Calista arrived he seemed genuine, kind even.

Skyler furrowed her brows as I walked into the family room. "What happened?"

I plunked down on the couch and bent over to take off my shoes. "Calista and her friends showed up while I was interviewing Cooper. Did you know that he and Calista are dating?"

Skyler sat next to me. Once my shoes were off, I peeled off my socks and wriggled my toes. "God, your feet stink." Skyler reeled back, plugging her nose. "You really need to start wearing sandals on hot days like this."

Without responding, I rolled my eyes. I was used to comments like this from her.

"I didn't think Calista and Cooper were dating," Skyler said, leaning her head back on the couch. "But I had heard that they hooked up."

"That's sort of what he said too." I sat up straight, pushing my hair out of my face.

"He shared his relationship status with you?"

I groaned inwardly, remembering how I pointedly asked him if Calista was his girlfriend. *Way to keep it professional, London.* "It just sort of came up in conversation." I waved away her question. "Anyway, it was no big deal. It was just an interview for the paper. I gotta say, you never seem to get this excited about my articles, Sky."

"That's because you don't usually interview Cooper Montgomery." She nudged me in the thigh. "You're so lucky. Every girl at our school wants to get close to him."

"I'm not close to him. I just asked him a few questions. That's it." I stretched out my legs and arms, feeling tired. If only Skyler would stop asking so many questions about Cooper. I loved Skyler. She was more like my sister than my friend, and she'd been there for me through a lot of shit. But Skyler was boy crazy, and I wasn't. Also, she'd always been fascinated by the popular crowd. Secretly I believed she wished she could be one of them.

She nodded. "So that's it, then? You're all finished?"

I bit my lip. "I will be after his game this weekend."

Her neck craned in my direction, her eyes like

daggers spearing into me. "You didn't say anything to me about having to attend his baseball game."

"I didn't know until today." The garage door sprung to life, signaling that Dad was home. I prayed that Skyler would let this drop when Dad came inside.

She shook her head. "I don't know how you put up with John. Every time he tells you to jump, you jump, no questions asked. And he acts like he runs the freaking New York Times or something. Not a measly school paper." She stopped herself, an apologetic look on her face. "No offense."

"None taken." I assured her. "Besides, it wasn't John who told me about the game. It was Cooper."

"Cooper invited you to his baseball game?" Her eyes bugged out so far I worried they would leap from her face.

"Baseball game?" Dad stepped into the room, his large frame casting a shadow over us. I definitely got my slight frame from my mom. Car grease stained Dad's meaty hands, grey shirt and black pants. His forehead was slick, his dark hair moist at the ends that curled slightly around his face. If I thought I was burning up at school, it was nothing compared to how hot it got at the auto shop where Dad worked. "I know I must have heard wrong. My pumpkin doesn't go to baseball games."

I cringed at Dad's nickname for me. He'd called me that ever since I was a little girl when I had an affinity for the color orange. There was an entire year when I refused to wear an outfit unless it had the color orange on it. My attempts at trying to get

20

him to stop calling me that were futile. And because I loved him so much, I let it slide.

"It's for an article," I explained.

"Cooper Montgomery, the star pitcher of our team, invited her." Skyler grinned.

"Is that so?" Dad's smile was a little wary. My 'no dating' stance was something Dad staunchly supported.

"Just because I know nothing about baseball. I think he wants to make sure I don't screw up the article," I explained, and Dad's face relaxed.

"Or maybe he wants to see you again," Skyler teased.

I ignored her. "Dinner is ready, Dad. I just have to warm up some tortillas when you want to eat."

"Great. I'll go get changed and be back in a jiffy." Only my dad used the word 'jiffy'. It was one of many outdated words he still sprinkled in everyday conversation.

"I should head home." Skyler stood.

"You can stay for dinner if you want," I offered.

"I wish, but I promised Mom I'd help her with dinner tonight," she responded, heading to the front door.

I nodded with understanding. Skyler's mom was always making her do some chore or another. She had two brothers, but her mom didn't expect them to do anything. The double standard pissed Skyler off, and I totally empathized. It would bother me too. Luckily, I didn't have any siblings. However, I'd give anything to have my mom back. I'd do

21

nothing but chores for the rest of my life if it meant she could still be here.

My gaze involuntarily swept over to the framed picture of her on the wall. Her blond hair was swept back from her face, her smile large and inviting. As I stared at it, the picture morphed right before my eyes like a funhouse mirror at the fair. Her face grew pale, her lips turned blue, her eyes widened in terror. I closed my eyes to stop the rest of the image from emerging, but it was too late. The recollection had started, and once that happened I could never stop it. Pretty soon all I saw was red.

Red everywhere.

Blood.

It's how I remembered her now. Tainted in blood.

CHAPTER 4
Cooper

I spotted Grandpa trimming the hedges when I pulled up in the driveway in my Honda civic. Hip hop music blasted from the speakers, and the silence was startling when I cut the engine. Reaching for my baseball bag, I snatched it off the passenger seat and then got out of the car.

After slamming the door shut, I held up my arm to get Grandpa's attention. "Grandpa."

He turned, a smile springing to his face. "Hey, son." Lowering the clippers, he walked in my direction. At sixty-five year's old, his hair was fully grey now. When I was younger it was dark brown to match his dark eyes. He wore a pair of plaid shorts and a blue shirt, tennis shoes on his feet. "How was practice?"

"It went well." I nodded, tucking my thumb under the strap of my bag. Grandpa played baseball when he was younger, and it was still his favorite sport. He told me once that when he was a kid he dreamt of playing professionally. I'd never seen him play, but Grandma told me he was pretty damn good. And I loved that I could talk baseball with him so openly. He'd always been my biggest supporter. "My bullpen went well, I hit all my spots, and all my pitches were moving."

"That's great." He slapped me on the back

with his free hand. It stung a little. Grandpa sometimes forgot his own strength. Sure he was getting older, but he was still strong and healthy. I hoped he'd always stay that way. Losing him or grandma wasn't even an idea I allowed myself to entertain. "I can't wait until the game on Saturday."

"Yeah, it should be a good one."

"I think dinner's about ready. Why don't you go on inside and get cleaned up? I'll be in in just a few minutes." Stepping away from me, he lifted the clippers.

Whirling around, I hurried inside. Icy air spilled from the air conditioning vents, and it felt good against my hot skin. After dropping my bag by the front door, I followed the scent of food and the sound of dishes clinking together until I located Grandma in the kitchen. She was bent over a pot on the stove, stirring with a large spatula. Her dark hair was pulled into a bun on the top of her head, and an apron was wrapped around her waist.

"Hey, Grandma." I swooped down to plant a quick kiss on her cheek, inhaling the familiar scent of lavender that always clung to her skin.

"How was your practice?" She turned to me, setting down the spatula.

"It went well."

"That's my boy." She patted my cheek.

She wasn't as interested in all the details as Grandpa was, but she supported me and attended all my games, so that's all that mattered.

"Dinner will be ready in about ten minutes," she said, returning her attention to the stove. Picking back up the spatula, she stirred the contents of the

24

pot. Steam rose from it, swirling around her face.

"Great. I'll hit the shower and be down in a few."

Grandma nodded as I headed upstairs. I passed the wall of framed family pictures and collages on the way to my room. Before reaching it, I felt my cell phone buzzing from the back pocket of my pants. Reaching behind me, I yanked it out.

Nate: Was it painful?

I smiled, reading my friend's text. He didn't have to clarify what he was talking about. I had been complaining to him about the article before practice today.

Me: It wasn't that bad.

Nate: I saw Calista walking toward the field after practice. How did that go?

My door was open, so I stepped inside my room and dropped onto my bed. Baseball players stared at me from the posters tacked all over my walls. The blinds on my large window were open, natural light streaming in and brightening the room.

Me: You know Calista.

And he did. He'd hooked up with her at the beginning of the school year.

Nate: Seriously, dude. She's a piece of work.

My stomach balling, I dropped the phone on my bed. After flinging off my shoes, I shuffled across the hallway to the bathroom. I peeled off my sweaty baseball clothes and then discarded them on the floor. Then I tossed my hat onto the counter before turning on the shower. My blond hair was damp from sweat. As I stepped into the shower, I caught my reflection in the mirror to see that chunks of my hair stuck out all over my head. It reminded me of London's hair when the wind kicked it up. She didn't bother smoothing it down. The girls I dated had a hissy fit when the wind messed with their perfectly styled hair. But she was nothing like the girls I dated. She was nothing like any girl I'd ever met. And I wasn't sure that was a good thing. Frankly, she was kind of annoying, all business-like and kind of rude.

Oh, well. It's not like I was going to have to spend much time with her. We'd finish the interview on Saturday and that would be it. And that was fine by me. It wasn't like I would ever voluntarily hang out with London. As I squirted some shampoo into my palm, my mind flew back to London's introduction, causing an involuntary chuckle to rise in my throat. She acted like a reporter for a freaking national publication or something. Clearly that chick had no idea how to loosen up.

Once I finished my shower, I went back into my room to change. After throwing on a pair of shorts and a t-shirt, my phone lit up on my bed. Glancing down at it, I saw that I had another text from Nate.

Nate: Can I get a ride with u to the party tomorrow night?

Me: I'm not going.

Nate: What? Last week u said u were.

Me: But now we have a game on Saturday.

Our games were typically on Monday and Wednesday afternoons, but yesterday's game got rained out, so it was moved to Saturday.

Nate: U need to loosen up, man.

Hadn't I thought the same thing about London just

26

a few minutes ago? Without responding, I left the phone on my bed and headed downstairs. Nate and I had this conversation all the time. He liked baseball, but it wasn't his life the way it was mine. And I had no desire to get into it with him again. It's funny, because what first drew me to Nate was his carefree attitude, his fun-loving nature. We had become friends our freshman year when we both made the baseball team. He was a hell of a third baseman, and a pretty damn good guy. But he didn't live and breathe the game the way I did. In fact, I knew very few people who did. Most of my friends were into partying and hooking up with chicks. Not that I didn't like that too. I did. And I went out when I could. I loosened up when I wanted to. But never on a night before a game.

The guys had a hard time understanding that, and I knew they'd harass me like crazy about my absence at the party. But when they showed up on Saturday morning with hangovers and played like shit, then I'd be the one laughing. Of course they wouldn't care. In their minds it would all be worth it. Besides, in their minds it wasn't a big deal since it was only fall ball. But for me, playing like shit wasn't an option, even if it was only the fall season. No way was I going to screw up my chance of playing for a good college next year. I had to be on my game at all times.

Baseball wasn't my hobby. It was my present, my future, my everything.

CHAPTER 5
London

I forgot to set my alarm clock.

It was the light peeking in through the blinds that finally woke me. My eyes popped open, and I stared around my room. However, I couldn't make anything out because I didn't have on my glasses or contacts. Throwing out my arm, my fingers fumbled around on my nightstand, brushing over my Kindle and my cellphone before finally touching my glasses. Closing my fingers around them, I plucked them up and brought them to my face. After placing them over my eyes, I blinked as the room came into focus. When my gaze fell to my alarm clock, my stomach plummeted. I only had twenty minutes to get to the game. Shit. It took almost that long to ride my bike. I could ask Dad for the car, but he probably had things to do today. And I had no desire for him to drive me to the game. The last time he dropped me off at school he hollered "I love you," at the top of his lungs as I scurried away from the car. Kids teased me for weeks, yelling, "I love you" as I passed them in the hall and making kissy faces at me. As if they didn't have enough reasons to make fun of me. It's not like I needed to give them any more ammunition.

I wanted to be angry with Dad, but I knew he didn't mean to embarrass me. It was just how he was. Still, I didn't want a repeat performance.

Hopping out of bed, I ran to my dresser. I still couldn't believe how late I overslept. Then again, I had been up late last night. I had started a new novel, and I couldn't put it down. In fact, I'd wanted to stay up until I finished it, but eventually I couldn't keep my eyes open any longer. Peering over my shoulder, I spotted my Kindle, and longing filled me. If only I could stay home and finish my book instead of having to go to this damn game. Nerves filled me at the thought. But I didn't have a choice. I had to turn in the article this week.

Grabbing the first outfit I could find, I snatched it out. It was a long-sleeved shirt and jeans, pretty much what I wore every day. *You might want to wear something different on Saturday.* Cooper's words floated through my mind, and I glanced down at the outfit I clutched in my hands. Dropping the shirt, I perused my drawer until I found a short-sleeved t-shirt. It was navy blue with a silver heart on the front. I think I'd only worn it one time before.

After quickly changing, I caught my reflection in the mirror above my dresser. This dresser used to be my mom's. It was in our garage for a long time. A few years ago, Dad was going to get rid of it, but I begged him to fix it up and let me have it. We sanded it down and repainted it. Dad said it was because it needed to be redone, but I knew the truth. He didn't want to be reminded of her every time he came in my room. Not that I blamed him, exactly. I didn't either. The dresser with the ornate mirror attached looked nothing like it had before. We had changed it so much that we could almost pretend it had never belonged to Mom. Yet, I knew it was

29

hers. And that alone gave me comfort. I liked knowing that a part of her was right here with me.

My hair was tangled and messy. Several brown strands coiled around my face, springing up in the air as if I'd hair-sprayed them like that, while other chunks were literally plastered to my head. Glancing back at the clock, I groaned. I so did not have time to shower. Snatching up my brush, I ran it through my tangles. It got caught a couple of times, but I forced it through. Then I twisted it up into a bun and secured it with a hair-tie and a few bobby pins. It didn't look great, but it was as good as it was going to get today. I wanted to put in my contacts, but I didn't have time. Grunting in frustration, I stared at my thick-rimmed black glasses in the mirror. I'd been wearing contacts since middle school, and I rarely went anywhere in my glasses. But today I had no choice.

After brushing my teeth and slipping on a pair of tennis shoes, I snatched up my pad of paper and purse, then raced to the front door. Dad was sitting at the kitchen table, a steaming cup of coffee in front of him and the newspaper in his hands. In this digital age, my dad still embraced the good old days, as he called them. He enjoyed the old-fashioned newspaper. Said he liked the feeling of it between his fingers, liked the smell of it and the crinkly sound it made when he turned the page.

"Where are you off to?" He lifted his head, only his eyes visible behind the pages.

"The baseball game at my school."

Dad lowered the paper, his eyebrows jumping up. "That's right. Should've reminded me. I would've went with you."

Thank god I didn't. If I thought him dropping me off was embarrassing, I can't even imagine how mortifying it would be if he came with me. "That's okay, but I have to get moving. I'm already late."

"Take the car," Dad offered.

"Are you sure? The game may be a couple of hours."

"I'm not going anywhere. I've got my paper and sports on the television. I'm good here." Dad smiled.

"Thanks." Relief swept over me as I grabbed the keys off the kitchen counter. "I'll come home right after."

"Take your time." Dad brought the large black and white pages back up, obscuring his face, the papers rustling with the movement.

Fisting the keys in my hand, I opened the front door and hurried outside. The sun was out, and it was already warm. I was glad I had decided to wear the short-sleeved shirt. Besides, it wasn't so bad. It was still modest with its high scoop neck.

I drove as fast as I could to the school. By the time I pulled into the school parking lot I had a couple minutes to get to the game in time. Yanking my pad of paper and purse off the passenger seat, I closed the car door and locked it. Then I walked swiftly toward the baseball field. As I neared it, I was surprised with how many people were in the bleachers. I knew the football games were packed, but I didn't expect the baseball team to draw a crowd. I wasn't sure why, but suspected it had to do with how much the school pushed football above all our other sports.

The team was out on the field by the time I made it to the bleachers. The only seat on the home side was in the middle. As I climbed over to it, I lost my footing and stumbled a bit, almost falling in some old lady's lap. But she was friendly as her arm came up to stop my fall.

"Sorry," I mumbled, my face flaming.

"No problem, dear." She peered up at me through her wide-brimmed straw hat, her coral painted lips curving into a smile that was warm and kind.

Biting my lip, I righted myself and carefully made my way to the open space. Sighing, I sat down, grateful to be seated. This was precisely why I hated this kind of thing. Sitting at home reading a novel was safe. I placed my pad of paper in my lap and lowered my purse onto the bleachers next to my thigh. Lifting my head, I caught sight of Cooper standing on the mound wearing his Tigers' uniform and ball cap. As he stood up tall, bringing the ball in close to his chest, I found myself mesmerized. His expression was calculated, focused, the set of his jaw determined. The stands on our side were quiet as he readied himself for the pitch. When he threw the ball, I held my breath. Only when the umpire called the strike did I dare breathe. I'd never been a sports fan, but there was something about the way Cooper pitched that fascinated me.

Clapping ensued around me. The old woman who I almost fell on cupped her hand around her mouth and shouted, "All right, Coop. Great job."

The man sitting next to her placed his hand on her back, smiling brightly. I wondered if they were related to Cooper. Grandparents, maybe.

This time when Cooper pitched the ball the batter hit it. Only he didn't make it far because an outfielder retrieved it, threw it to first, and the runner was out. Cooper played well the remainder of the inning and pretty soon the umpire called three outs. Cooper jogged off the mound as the other Tigers players headed toward the dugout. I watched him jog, his cleats pounding on the grass. When he reached the dugout, his head bobbed up and he smiled into the bleachers. At first I thought he was smiling at me, and heat crept up into my cheeks. But then the older couple I'd wondered about waved and smiled in his direction. He grinned and nodded his head at them before returning his attention to his team. I was surprised at the obvious show of silent affection. It really messed with my image of Cooper as this cocky, selfish jock.

As I settled back in my seat, something bright pink aroused my attention. I glanced over to see Calista swaggering over to the bleachers wearing a tiny pink tank top, white shorts and tall wedges. On her head was the same ball cap she'd had on the other day. I whipped my head away from her and stared out at the field, hoping she didn't see me. The last thing I wanted to do was talk to Calista today. I wanted to finish this damn article and go back to my normal life. One that didn't include jocks and the popular crowd. One that was filled with the safety of the written word and the security of my imagination.

CHAPTER 6
Cooper

When I pitched, the rest of the world fell away. The crowd disappeared from my vision, the noises faded from my ears. I would forget other people existed outside of the field. It was just me, the batter, the ball, and my team. Outside of that, nothing else mattered. Nothing could rock me or upset my focus.

Until today.

I threw a pitch, striking out the batter, when I saw something out of the corner of my eye. Before the game had started I had seen where Grandma and Grandpa were sitting. Maybe that's why I noticed it, because the commotion was right where they had been seated. I glanced over when a girl wearing a wrinkled shirt and jeans, her hair in a messy bun, stumbled and almost fell on my grandma. My heart leapt with worry until Grandma caught her. Relieved, I exhaled. My mind flew back to last year when Grandma took a fall on the stairs of the front porch. Fortunately, she'd only suffered minor bruising and a sprained ankle, but it could have been a lot worse. Ever since then, I'd been warning her to be cautious. However, I never thought coming to one of my baseball games would be dangerous. What the hell was wrong with that girl? Was she drunk or something?

When she glanced up, I got a good look at

her face and recognized that it was London. Her cheeks were flushed, her expression one of embarrassment, and I felt a little bad for my judgmental thoughts. Clearly she hadn't meant to fall. I remembered her dropping her pen the first time I met her. Maybe she was klutzy. Now that I knew who it was, I was sure she wasn't drunk. Taking a deep breath, I turned back to the batter and forced myself to regain my focus.

Once I got back in the zone, I was able to stay there the remainder of the game. In fact, I was so locked in, I hadn't even noticed that Calista had shown up until the game ended. And then I wished I'd never noticed. She stood against the fence, her fingers twisted around the chain-links, smiling at me. My stomach churned at the fact that she was wearing my hat again. Seriously. Why didn't the chick pee on me to mark her territory? When our eyes locked, she smiled largely.

"Hey, Cooper!" Her voice was so loud I feared the school across town could hear her. As it was, most of the parents in the stands looked over, including my grandparents. They weren't stupid. They knew I dated lots of girls, and they were kind enough to let me be. As long as I got good grades and kept up with my practicing, they sort of let me do what I wanted. I'd yet to screw up, so it worked out.

Still, I didn't want Calista acting like my girlfriend in front of them like this. I didn't really bring girls home to meet them. There wasn't any point. When I did introduce them to a girl, I wanted her to be someone special. Someone I could see myself with long term. And I knew that wouldn't happen for years. I assumed it wouldn't happen until I was playing professional ball. It sure as hell wouldn't be while I was still in high school. And it sure as hell wouldn't be Calista.

After the huddle with our coach, Nate approached me. His eyes were bloodshot, dark rings around them. He'd played pretty shitty, but somehow we'd still won the game, so I wasn't that upset with him.

"Fun time last night, huh?" I teased.

"The best. You should've come."

"And play the way you did? No thanks. I wanted to win this game."

"Shut up," Nate said, but a smile played on his lips. "I didn't play that bad."

I chuckled, not bothering to correct him.

He nodded in the direction of Calista still pressed against the fence, staring in our direction. "Looks like you haven't talked to her yet."

My insides twisted. "No, not yet."

"She was at the party last night."

Hope unfurled at his words. Perhaps she'd hooked up with another guy. That would make this so much easier. "Really?"

"Yep, and she was wearing that damn hat and telling everyone that you two were together."

"Shit," I muttered under my breath. *I was screwed.*

Nate laughed, slapping me on the back. "It's not that bad. She's hot, and hella eager. You could hold on to her a little longer."

I felt sick at his words. She wasn't a toy. She

was a person. Then again, I supposed I wasn't treating her any better. I'd been stringing her along and using her, hadn't I? Just because I didn't verbalize it didn't make it any better. "Nah, I can't do that. Not if she thinks we're a couple." *Damn, how did I let this get so out of control?*

Trudging away from Nate, I made my way toward Calista. As I approached, I caught site of London sitting in the bleachers, that damn pad of paper in her lap. *Shit.* I had forgotten about her. My gaze sweeping the area around me, I didn't see Grandma or Grandpa. Most likely they'd already left. Usually they took off right after the game, and we talked later. I found myself relieved by this. That way I wouldn't have to introduce them to Calista. It would make what I had to say a little easier.

"Hey, Coop." Calista leaned in, her lips almost touching the fence.

I cringed at her using my nickname. It was what the guys on the team called me, not the girls I fooled around with. I didn't know why it bothered me so much, but it did. I didn't like the way it sounded coming out of her mouth.

My eyes lifted to the hat nestled in her curls. "Still wearing my hat, huh?"

"I never take it off," she said. "Well, except when I sleep…and shower." She winked.

Now I was picturing her naked, soap lathered all over her smooth flesh. *Shit.*

Reaching through the fence, she drug her nail up my arm. "You played great today."

"Oh, yeah?" Despite my best efforts, my flirty side came out to play. It was like I couldn't even control it.

"Yeah." She leaned in close. "I may even have a reward for you."

My pulse quickened. Maybe Nate was right. I didn't have to break it off with her today. The bleachers creaked as London stood up behind Calista. Once again, I'd forgotten about her. *Damn it, what was wrong with me?* As if in response to my internal question, Calista's fingers tickled the sensitive flesh of my arm, trailing up under my sleeve. London stomped down the stairs, the hard look on her face betraying her impatience.

I cleared my throat. "Um…how about I catch up to you later, Calista? I sort of have a meeting right now."

"Meeting?" She furrowed her brows, appearing perplexed. Not as if that was uncommon. She always seemed a little confused.

"Well, interview, actually. For the paper. Remember?"

Irritation flared in her eyes as she whirled around to where London was standing in the grass. "Oh. Right." She scrunched up her nose in disgust. "I wondered what she was doing here."

London spun around, her back to us.

"London, wait!" I called to her, feeling bad. I was the one who asked her to come here, after all. "I'll be there in a minute."

Her shoulders stiffened, and she stopped walking. Before she could take off again, I flashed Calista an apologetic look. "I'll text you later?"

"Promise?" The hopeful look in her eyes made me feel like shit. Then my gaze lowered to her boobs, barely confined in her top, and the remorse left me. I mean, she's the one who wanted this, right? I was actually doing her a favor.

"Promise." I smiled.

She drew her hand back, and turned around. "Don't leave me hanging, Cooper," she called over her shoulder.

I stared at her ass while she sashayed away.

"You sure she's not your girlfriend?" London asked.

Shrugging, I maneuvered around the fence. "I didn't think you came here to talk about my personal life."

London had the decency to look ashamed. "Point taken." By the time I reached her, she was scanning her pad of paper, her eyes moving swiftly behind her glasses. I didn't remember her wearing glasses the last time we talked. "I have a few more questions, and then we'll be done."

"Sounds good." I didn't mean to sound so enthusiastic about it, and I saw a flicker of annoyance in London's eyes. "Wanna sit?" The bleachers and field had pretty much cleared out. Only a few stragglers were left, and I needed to sit down. Weariness was settling on me, blanketing my muscles.

We both sat on the first bleacher and it moaned beneath us. The sun was strong, and sweat gathered under my hat and down my spine. I noticed that London had worn a short-sleeved shirt today. She still had on those damn jeans though. I had no idea why the girl chose to torture herself with the clothes she wore. But it was none of my business, so

39

I let it go.

London pulled a pen out of her purse, her head still bent over her notebook. A few strands of brown hair escaped from her bun, hanging against her face. One strand curled around her thick glasses. Her cheeks were red, and I assumed it was from the heat.

"I guess first I should congratulate you on the win," London spoke, cutting through my thoughts.

"Thanks."

"Your number has always been eleven. Is there a reason for that?"

Her question surprised me. She'd clearly done her research. Yeah, the number had significance, but only a few people knew about it. I certainly wasn't going to share it with the whole school. "Nope," I lied. "Just like the number."

"I noticed you get really in the zone when you're out there," she observed.

I nodded, unsure of what to say. It didn't really seem like a question.

"There was only one time where you even seemed to notice the crowd."

My stomach knotted. Did she see me looking when she fell?

"It was in between innings when you smiled at the older couple sitting in front of me. Are they relatives of yours?"

I raised a brow, surprised by the personal question. What did my grandparents have to do with baseball? But I decided to answer anyway. What could it hurt? "Yeah. They're my grandparents."

"Do they come to your games often?"

"Almost every single one." I smiled.

"Really?"

"Yeah. My grandpa used to play ball when he was younger. They enjoy coming to the games."

"Is he the reason you love baseball?"

I shook my head. "Um…no. Not really." Holding my breath, I prayed she wouldn't continue to pry.

"So it was just your parents who encouraged you to play then?"

I was grateful that she worded it that way. All I had to do was nod.

"Were they here today? I didn't see your grandparents talking with anyone else."

"Um…" I scratched the back of my neck, finding it difficult to draw breath. "No, they weren't."

"Oh." She opened her mouth like she was going to ask another question, and panic bloomed inside of me.

"Look, it's really hot, and I've been out here since early this morning. Can we try to wrap this up?"

She reeled back, looking stricken.

"Sorry," I muttered, wishing I hadn't been so harsh with her. But damn it, why did she have to be so nosy about my personal life? I thought we were supposed to stick to baseball. "I'm just exhausted."

Her expression softened, and her shoulders relaxed. "That makes sense. You did work hard today." She scribbled something on her pad of paper. "I actually think I have all I need in order to write the article."

41

"Okay." I stood, relieved to be finished.

"Thanks for letting me interview you." She stood too. "Do you want to see a copy of the article before it goes live?"

"Nah. I trust you." I winked, and pink rose on her cheeks. Seriously, I needed to reign in my flirting. She was the last girl I wanted to give the wrong impression too. It was bad enough that I had Calista breathing down my neck.

"All right. Then I guess I'll see ya around." Her eyes shifted nervously behind her glasses.

"Yeah. See ya."

She turned to walk away, and I went in search of my bag. Knowing that the interview was over, it was like having a weight lifted off my shoulders. I hadn't even realized how worried I was about it until now. The entire time she interviewed me it was like this ball of nerves sat right in my gut. I thought I had been irritated about it because it was a waste of time. But now I knew it was more than that. I had been worried about the questions. Concerned that she would somehow find out about my parents. And that was something I didn't want to talk about.

CHAPTER 7
London

It was late Sunday afternoon when I finished writing the article. I would've finished it earlier, but when I came back from the game yesterday I ended up taking a nap. Normally I didn't sleep in the middle of the day, but maybe all the heat had gotten to me. Then last night I got engrossed in my latest novel, so I didn't start working on the article until today. Sitting at the desk in my room, I read back over it. First, I had summarized the baseball game and described Cooper's pitching style. Then I went into some of our interview. While reading over Cooper's responses, I pictured his face, how it lit up whenever he talked about baseball. Surprisingly, he had almost the same expression when he talked about his grandparents. Rarely did I meet guys like that, and it confused me.

It was like Cooper had a split personality or something. On the one hand he was a doting grandson, passionate about baseball. I knew from the research I'd done that he got straight A's in school too. That Cooper, the one that I felt drawn too while interviewing, was straight laced, the perfect student and all around good guy. But the other side of Cooper was the one I'd been familiar with all throughout high school. He was arrogant and rude, a flirt, a player, a partier. I may not have been

43

Calista's biggest fan, but I was still disgusted by how easily he dismissed her at both practice and the game. Clearly they had some kind of relationship by the way she was acting, and it bothered me that he brushed it off as nothing.

It was hard for me to reconcile these two sides of Cooper. That's why I stuck to the subject of baseball in the article and didn't allow my personal feelings to interfere. I wasn't sure who Cooper truly was, but when he spoke of baseball I felt like he seemed authentic and real, so that's how I portrayed him. I didn't mention his grandparents, but I did add in what he told me about his mom saying that he was born with a baseball in his hand. I thought it added a nice touch.

My handwriting was so atrocious there were a few words I had to read repeatedly before understanding what it said. As I snatched up the article and stood, I wished for the umpteenth time that we had a computer here. We used to have an old desktop, but it crashed last year and we'd yet to purchase a new one. Dad was out running errands, so I'd have to ride my bike to the library to type up the article. Stretching, I let out a yawn. My bed was calling to me, but I shook away the thoughts. Why was I so damn tired lately? I thought about how the flu was going around at school, and I silently prayed I wouldn't get it. I made a mental note to take some vitamin C later, as I headed outside.

The air was even warmer than it was this morning, and I was already wiping sweat off my forehead when I jumped on my bike and pedaled down my driveway. By the time I reached the street,

I was grateful that Skyler hadn't spotted me. If she had, she'd offer for me to use her computer. Not that I wouldn't appreciate it, but it was so loud at Skyler's house. Her brothers were rowdy, and her parents were talkative. I was used to quiet, so it was all a little much for me.

I rounded the corner and guided my bike up on the sidewalk. Pedaling swiftly, I passed a man watering his grass and a group of kids playing in their front yard. A woman that I assumed was their mom sat on the front porch, a magazine spread over her lap. My heart pinched at the scene. I remembered my mom sitting on the porch watching me play when I was younger. She had the best smile. My dad used to say that it wasn't just her lips that smiled, it was her whole face. I'd never met anyone else filled with such genuine joy and kindness. In the end, it was her undoing.

And that's why I was so guarded, careful to never be too friendly, too trusting. Skyler often told me I had "resting bitch face," and I think she meant it as a criticism. But I took it as a compliment. That "resting bitch face" was my defense mechanism. If only my mom had used it, maybe she'd still be here.

Shaking away the thoughts, I took a deep breath and pedaled harder. Thoughts like this weren't helping. No amount of wishing could bring her back. If it could, she would have returned years ago. I can't tell you how many nights I lie in bed after she left us, prayers for her return tumbling from my lips. The words lingered in the air, desperate wishes scrawled in invisible ink. I prayed they would reach her and yank her back to me. Yet, every morning when I awoke, she was still gone.

Nearing the next street, I readied myself to turn. The library was only one block down now. A breeze feathered over my skin, soft, like silk. A car was parked up on the sidewalk blocking my path, so I swerved around it. My bike sloped downward until my tires hit the asphalt. A car came up behind me so I moved as far to the right as I could. After passing the parked vehicle, I steered toward the sidewalk once again preparing to slide back up onto it. Only I lost my balance for a minute and my tire hit the side at a funny angle. My bike froze, my body pitching forward. I squeezed on the handlebars attempting to right myself, but it was too late. My bike was toppling over, my body with it. As a last-ditch effort, I threw my arms out in order to cushion my fall. My palms hit the sidewalk first, my skin stinging. By the time the rest of my body followed, I was so tangled in my bike I felt the chain cut into my leg. My ankle rolled and pain shot up through my calf. The handlebars smacked me in the face, but luckily my head didn't hit the ground. Somehow I kept it up. Even though I was wearing a helmet, I didn't want to chance it.

A car pulled up next to where I fell, and I groaned. I was so not in the mood for a Good Samaritan right now. They probably thought they were helping, but what I really wanted was to be left alone. I could deal with this on my own. Sitting up, I attempted to peel the bike off. That's when I noticed how badly I'd scraped my palms. Blood oozed from the lines painted in my flesh. The straps from my backpack slid down my shoulders and arms. I shrugged it off, and it dropped onto the sidewalk.

46

My breath hitching in my throat, I turned away, warding off the unwanted memories. Blood always did this. It made me think of that day. The one day I never wanted to think of again.

"You okay?"

My head snapped up at the familiar voice, and I hoped I was wrong about who it was. One look and my suspicion was confirmed. *Shit*. Could this day get any worse?

"London?"

"Hi, Cooper," I responded calmly as if I wasn't lying on the ground wrapped around my bicycle and covered in blood and bruises. Reaching up, I adjusted the helmet on my head which had slipped down to my eyes. That's probably why he didn't recognize me when he first pulled up. If he had, I was sure he wouldn't have stopped. He probably thought there was some hot chick under this helmet. Boy was he wrong.

"Here, let me help you up." He bent down, his arms extended toward me.

I waved him away. "It's fine. I got it." Shifting, I attempted to shove the bike off and stand up, but it was more difficult than I first anticipated. Not to mention that the pain in my ankle was worsening. Biting my lip, I tried one more time.

Ignoring my protests, Cooper grabbed the bike and lifted it off of me carefully. Then he propped it up on the kickstand and turned back to me. "Can you stand?"

"Of course I can stand," I barked. "I mastered the art of standing years ago."

An amused look passed over his features.

Irritated, I set my hands on the ground and pushed my body up. My body trembled a little as I reached a standing position. I teetered over as I tried to put weight on my ankle. As my body swayed to the side, Cooper's arms came up to steady me.

"Whoa." His grip around my middle was firm, yet oddly gentle. His touch sent an unwanted chill up my spine, but I was afraid to push away. Afraid I would fall over. I was already mortified enough, I didn't need to add to it. "I better take a look at that ankle."

Blowing out a breath, I hesitantly agreed. The last thing I wanted was for Cooper to examine my ankle. In fact, what I wanted was for him to leave and forget this whole thing happened. But I wasn't sure how I'd get home if he left. I couldn't even stand on my damn ankle.

With his arm still around my waist, he helped me to the ground. Then he knelt beside me and lifted the bottom of my jeans to expose my ankle. The wind kicked up, and the scent of mint and spice wafted under my nose, causing my heart to race. Cooper's fingers trailed over my flesh as he lowered my sock to get a better look. I shivered.

"It doesn't look too good." He frowned. "Can you move it?"

With a little effort I was able to bend it. "Yeah."

"It's probably not broken then, just sprained. But it's swelling a lot already." His hand remained fixated on my skin. It was warm and soft. I hated to admit it, but it felt good. He glanced up at me, and his face was so close to mine that if I moved forward our noses would touch. Unnerved, I drew back a little. "Do you live near here?"

"Um…" Fear took root in my stomach. "Why?"

A smile flickered. "Don't worry. I'm not planning on stalking you, but I do need to get you home." He glanced over at my bike, and then his eyes made their way to my ankle. "Unless you plan to ride back."

My cheeks flamed at how silly and paranoid I was being. There was no way I was going to get myself home. I did need his help. Then again, Dad was probably home by now. He could pick me up. "It's okay. I can have my dad get me." Unzipping the backpack sitting next to me, I fished my hand inside. It was then that I pictured my phone sitting on the desk in my room. Damn it, I'd forgotten it. "Never mind." I sighed. "I forgot my phone." Embarrassed, I lifted my hand, wiping my face. Too late I realized that was not a smart move since my hands were streaked in blood.

Without skipping a beat, Cooper reached out and swiped his finger across my cheek. I froze, my heart picking up speed. No guy had ever touched my face before. When our eyes met, he cleared his throat. "You had a little blood on your face," he said, nervous laughter under his words.

I nodded as he pulled his hand away. "My house is around the corner." Reaching over, I zipped back up my backpack and then grabbed it, clutching the straps in between my fingers.

"Okay." Sliding his hands under my armpits, he hoisted me up and then guided me to his car.

After getting in the passenger seat, I peered over at my bike. Then I looked behind me at the backseat of his compact car.

"What are we gonna do with my bike?"

Cooper smiled, that damn dimple forming on his cheek again. If only he could put that thing away. It would make it easier to dislike him. "Lucky for you, I have a bike rack on top of my car."

"Do you ride?"

"Sometimes. My grandpa and I used to ride the trails on the weekends before baseball season started back up." After closing the passenger door, he walked toward my bike. Settling back in the seat, I thought about what a strange turn of events this was. What were the chances that Cooper would be my Good Samaritan? More importantly, what were the chances that I would actually be happy about it?

CHAPTER 8
Cooper

After securing London's bike to the top of the car, my cell buzzed inside my pocket. Before even looking at it, I knew who it was. I had been on my way to Calista's when I saw London fall. It's why I was driving through this part of town. This street was a shortcut between my house and Calista's, and I knew if it took too long to get to her house my conscience would take over and I'd never make it there. After the game yesterday I'd ended up hanging out with the guys until late last night. But that didn't stop Calista from texting nonstop. I knew it was a mistake to hook up with her again, but I hadn't been thinking with my brain when I got in my car earlier. Calista was persuasive, I'd give her that.

When I saw the girl fall on her bike, I had no idea it was London. All I knew was that it was a nasty fall. I'd had a fall like that once, and if no one had stopped for me, I would've been screwed. The difference was that I had actually broken my leg. That's why I pulled over. Several cars passed by as if they hadn't even seen the crash. But it was impossible to miss, so I knew they had seen it. People's ability to be selfish and ignore other people's needs never ceased to amaze me. As badly as I was itching to get to Calista's, I couldn't pass by a person in need like that.

Now I was glad I had pulled over. London may be a total pain in the ass, but I would've felt like shit if she was stuck here all night with a sprained ankle. It was clear she was untrusting. And let's face it, the chick was a mess. Who else would help her? Even though I was pretty sure she didn't like me that much, at least I wasn't a stranger. I had a feeling she would never let a stranger drive her home. It was like pulling teeth to get her to say yes to me.

As I walked toward the driver's side door, I glanced down at my phone.

Calista: Where r u?

Me: Something came up.

Calista: U r still coming over, right?

I stared through the window at London sitting in the passenger seat. She was holding her ankle, her face contorted in pain. She'd taken her helmet off, and it sat in her lap. Her golden hair was disheveled, a sweaty, tangled knot at the nape of her neck. She must have felt me staring because she craned her neck, her eyes catching mine. Then she flashed me a pained, yet grateful smile. It was the most vulnerable I'd seen her, and it took me aback.

Me: I don't think so.

Without waiting for a response, I shoved the phone back into my pants pocket and slid into the car. I needed to get London home so she could ice her ankle.

"Where to?" I asked, after turning on the engine.

"Turn around," she instructed.

I did as I was told, and slowly moved down the street.

"Then turn right at this stop sign."

I flicked on my blinker and slowed. After turning, we passed an apartment complex and a few duplexes. Rarely did I come over to this part of town, and it was unfamiliar.

"My house is right here." She pointed with her index finger at a rundown duplex. The paint was chipped, the grass yellow. By the way she bent her head and bit her lip, it was clear that she was ashamed of it. Now I wondered if her hesitation of me coming over had more to do with pride than fear.

As I pulled up along the curb, I nodded and pasted on a smile, determined to make her feel comfortable. The driveway was empty, the house dark. "Is anyone home?"

She shook her head. "I thought Dad would be home by now, but it doesn't look like it."

"Then I'll help you inside." After shutting off the engine, I maneuvered around the car, opened her door and reached for her. As I secured my arm around her waist, I caught a whiff of apple scent. It floated from her hair that was slowly falling out of the knot she had it in. Tendrils broke loose and whipped in the wind. Her fingers closed around my shirt, her eyes colliding with mine. They were light brown, the color of caramel, but with yellow flecks, like tiny pieces of gold. For a moment I was mesmerized by them. I paused, getting lost in them as if spellbound. A dog barked in the distance, and the spell was broken. Unsure what the hell happened, I averted my gaze and moved forward. She was walking a little more stable, her ankle able to support her slight frame better than before. But she still needed my support to get into the house.

The interior of London's duplex was nicer than the exterior. It was cozy, even, with old fashioned furniture and warm paintings on the wall. After lowering London into the dark leather recliner near the front door, I asked her if she had an ice pack.

"You really don't have to do all this," she said, dropping her backpack on the ground. "My dad should be home any minute. Or I can text Skyler, my neighbor, and she can come over. You can go, really. You've done enough already."

She was unlike any other girl I'd ever met. Most girls would be begging me for help and attention at this point. She was practically pushing me away. And her ankle was swelling by the minute. She must be in extreme pain, yet she was calm and collected. Not at all like someone who just had a crash on their bike. Not to mention the fact that she scraped up her hands pretty badly too. For some reason her insistence that she could handle this on her own only made me want to help her more.

"I'm not leaving you like this," I said firmly. "You're a mess."

"Gee, thanks." She stuck out her bottom lip in a pout. It was the flirtiest gesture I'd seen from her, and it stirred a strange feeling inside. One I didn't want to have. One I refused to even acknowledge. "But since you insist on helping, there's an ice pack in the freezer."

Nodding, I walked into the kitchen. After locating an ice pack and wetting a rag, I headed back into the family room. Kneeling down in front of London, I untied her shoe and carefully slipped it off.

Then I gently placed the ice pack over her ankle. Afterward, I asked her to hold out her palms. Her eyes grew serious as she extended her arms, palm sides up. Dragging the rag over her palms, I rubbed gently, erasing all traces of dried blood.

"Is that better?" I asked.

She nodded, her lips pressed together.

With my fingers around her wrists, I inspected her hands. "Do you have a first aid kit? You should probably clean out these cuts and put on some bandaids."

"It's fine. I can do that later." In one swift movement, she drew her hands back. Tucking them up into her body, she lowered her head.

Taking my cue, I stood back up. It was probably time to go anyway. I did have somewhere to be after all. And I should have wanted to leave. I had a sexy girl waiting. A girl who had told me in graphic detail what she wanted to do with me. But for some reason I was hesitant to leave London. My gaze landed on her backpack, and I knew I was stalling. *What had gotten into me?*

"Why did you have your backpack with you on your bike ride? Planning to take a break to do homework?" I teased.

She sighed. "Actually, I was on my way to the library to type up your article. Now it won't be done in time."

I felt like an ass. This girl lived such a different life than mine. I thought of my nice suburban neighborhood, and two story house. Of the two computers we owned and the laptop sitting in the backseat of my car. *My laptop.* Of course.

55

"Hey, I have a laptop in my car. Wanna use it?"

She shook her head. "Oh, no. It's okay. I'll figure it out."

Her stubbornness was sort of endearing at first, but now it was kind of annoying. Why couldn't the chick take any help? "C'mon. It's not like you're going anywhere on that ankle tonight."

"God, you're persistent. Anyone ever tell you that?"

I chuckled. "I have heard that before. Yes."

She sighed. "Well, since you clearly don't know how to take no for an answer, then I guess I have no choice."

"Now you're finally seeing reason," I bantered back as I stepped toward the door. "I'll be right back, and I'll grab your bike while I'm at it."

"You can leave it by the garage." Her lips curved slightly at the edges. "Thanks," she practically whispered the word, and I wondered why this was so hard for her.

"Sure." Reaching for the knob, I turned it and stepped outside. As I walked toward my car, I caught movement out of the corner of my eye. A girl with dark hair stared at me through the neighbor's window. Her jaw dropped as if she was in shock at the sight of me, causing my stomach to coil.

Before the interview I hadn't remembered seeing London around school much. But the truth was, that I had. I just hadn't noticed her. She was always kind of in the background. A silent girl, her head bent downward, her hair obscuring her face. But there were times when our paths crossed. We had English class together last year, even though I was a year ahead of her in school. One day she tripped and fell on her way into class, and everyone teased her. For days the whispers and smart ass remarks circled.

And there was the list that Calista and her friends made last year. It was the kind of list no one wanted to grace. One of those derogatory lists, filled with mean things like "ugliest hair" and "girl that no one wants to kiss." London's name had been on it in several different categories. And I had the sick feeling she knew it too.

The surprised expression of the girl in the window was etched in my mind, causing me to realize why London was behaving the way she was. It wasn't pride or fear. It was uncertainty. It was doubt.

She wasn't used to people being nice to her.

CHAPTER 9
London

Cooper's laptop was nice, all sleek and chrome. Envy cropped up when I opened it and ran my fingers over the keyboard. Cooper plugged it in, so I didn't have to get up. A part of me wished he'd stop being so damn nice. Another part of me wanted him to stay here with me forever. I was so perplexed, my head spun. Trying to ignore the fact that Cooper was sitting on the couch in my living room watching me, I smoothed out my handwritten article and started typing. My hands trembled with each letter I touched. Feeling Cooper's eyes on me, my skin buzzed, warmth skating right under my flesh. Biting my lip, I continued to type, forcing myself to remain calm. But it was a losing battle. Nerves rattling, I kept fumbling the words, having to back up and retype almost every one after botching it. And it didn't help that my palms were covered in scratches. In order to not hurt them further, I had to hold my wrists up at a weird angle.

"How is your ankle?" Cooper asked.

"Better," I answered honestly, glancing down at the ice pack over it. "Of course it's numb, so maybe that's why."

Cooper chuckled. "Yeah, that'll help."

My hands stilled, pausing over the keys. What was Cooper still doing here? I couldn't figure it out.

The whole thing was baffling. It's not like we were friends or anything. "Why are you being so nice?" I blurted out.

Cooper's eyes widened, his mouth slacking. He looked stunned. The truth was, I sort of was too. I hadn't exactly meant to say that aloud. But now that I had, I was interested in the answer.

"I didn't realize I was usually such an ass." One side of Cooper's mouth curved upward.

"I didn't say you were an ass," I backpedaled, my gaze sweeping over the laptop covering my legs. I was the ass for putting him down when he'd rescued me today.

"Asking why I'm being nice today sort of implies that you don't think I normally am," he pointed out.

Unsure of what to say to make this better, I stared down at my hands. "Sorry," I finally mumbled.

"No, it's fine. I get it." Reaching up, he tugged lightly on the rim of his ball cap. "It makes sense why you'd ask that. We've never really hung out before."

His admission buoyed me. "We've never even talked before."

"Unless you count the interview." Cooper grinned. "Speaking of which, since I'm here, can I see what you wrote?"

"Um…sure. Let me just finish typing it. You'll never be able to read my handwriting." When I returned to the article, the sound of the garage door opening sounded behind me. Dad was home. Cooper must have heard the noise too, because he sat up straighter, his shoulders tensing. I typed swiftly, trying to finish fast.

The door leading from the kitchen into the garage popped open. "Pumpkin," Dad hollered, and I cringed.

"In here," I said between gritted teeth, unable to look up at Cooper. I was sure he was wearing a cheesy grin, laughing to himself. And I could hear the teasing at school tomorrow, everyone calling me pumpkin like it was the funniest shit ever. Why had I allowed Cooper to take me home? I wasn't in his group. We weren't friends. He was probably here to gain information to use against me. His damn dimples and easy grin had sucked me in. I was an idiot, plain and simple.

I heard the sound of bags being set down, and then Dad's feet shuffled on the hard floor. "Oh, sorry. I didn't know you had company." I detected the wariness in his tone. Not that I was surprised. This was the first time a boy had ever been in our home. In fact, it was the first time anyone other than Skyler had been here.

"Uh...yeah. It was sort of unexpected." I glanced over at Cooper. "Dad, this is Cooper. I fell off my bike, and he happened to be driving by at the same time."

"You fell off your bike?" Concern filled Dad's face. "Are you okay?" His gaze roved over my body until it rested on my ankle.

"It's not broken," Cooper interjected. "Not like I'm a doctor or anything, but I've broken bones before. She can bend it. I think it's just sprained."

I was surprised by Cooper's nervous rambling. I'd only ever seen him sure and confident.

Why was my dad making him anxious?

Dad lifted his head to Cooper. "Thanks for taking care of her." Taking a step forward, he extended his hand. "I'm Dexter, London's dad."

"Nice to meet you, Dexter." Cooper stood, took Dad's hand and shook it.

It was weird seeing the two of them together. Almost like it made this whole thing too real. Fantasies unleashed, and my heart squeezed. I couldn't allow my mind to go there. Cooper only felt pity for me. That's all this was. Besides, it's not like I'd ever want more from him. I wasn't interested in guys. Not right now. I wanted to stay safe here with my dad and my books, and to focus on my writing. That's it.

Dad's eyes slid up to Cooper's hat. "Oh, you must be the baseball player London was interviewing."

"That's me." Cooper beamed.

Hurriedly, I typed in the last few sentences. "All done," I said, triumphantly.

"Great. Can I take a look?" Cooper asked.

"Sure. Do you want to read it before I email it to John?"

Cooper paused. "Nah. I can take a look afterward."

"All right. Well, then I'll send it to him and save it to your laptop. That way you can look at it whenever you want." I told myself that I misread the look that crossed his face. It looked like disappointment, but that couldn't be right. I was sure he was beyond relieved to finally be able to get the hell out of here. Cooper could find a lot more riveting things to do than hang out with an injured nerd and her dad.

"Sounds good." He smiled, turning to my dad. "Looks like I'm outta here."

"Well, you're welcome to come back anytime," Dad said, shocking me further. This whole afternoon had been like an episode of the Twilight Zone. None of it made any sense. I half expected to wake up and find it was all some bizarre dream. "I'm going to go put away the stuff I bought at the store." Dad ducked out of the room. I heard the rustling of paper bags when he reached the kitchen.

After shooting off the email, I saved the document and then closed the laptop. Cooper unhooked the cord. Before picking up the laptop, his gaze landed on the framed picture of my mom on the wall.

"Is that your mom?" he asked.

I nodded, the air leaving me.

"You look exactly like her."

"Thanks," I muttered.

"Your dad seems nice. Too bad I didn't get to meet your mom." He reached for the laptop. "Maybe some other time."

I knew these were benign words, a way to fill up the silence, but they were personal. Too personal. It was one of the many reasons I didn't invite people over. Tears pricked at the corner of my eyes. I snorted. "Yeah, I don't think so."

"Why not?" With his hand on the laptop, his gaze slammed into mine.

Staring into his eyes, I exhaled.

"I don't know if you realize this, but you

have a pretty big chip on your shoulder. I'm trying to do something nice for you, and you're not exactly making it easy." After sliding the laptop off my lap, he tucked it under his arm.

"That's not what I meant." My eyes flickered to the picture. "She's gone. That's why you'll never meet her."

Cooper's face fell. "Oh, I'm so sorry."

"It's okay. You couldn't have known." *And I wish he didn't know now.* Again I mentally slapped myself for allowing him into my house and life like this. I'd done nothing but give him ammunition to use against me. *What the hell was I thinking?* As I said goodbye to him, the ramifications of what I'd done crashed over me. I knew it had been a mistake to allow him to come over.

And I had the strange feeling that nothing would ever be the same again.

A loud, repetitive screech sounded in the distance. But it was far away. So far I couldn't reach it. My body floated in nothingness, like I was lying on a cloud.

"London? London?"

I stirred at Dad's insistent voice. "Huh?" Groggy, I rolled over in bed.

The annoying noise ceased. "Your alarm was going off for like ten minutes. Are you going deaf?" Dad joked, his finger poking my ear gently. "Do you need to get your ears checked?"

"No, I can hear just fine." I sat up in bed, reaching for my glasses. The edges of the bandaids on my palms caught on the nightstand, pulling at my skin. "I was deep asleep, I guess."

"Don't know how you could sleep through that awful noise. You feeling all right?"

"Yeah. Just tired." I put on my glasses, and Dad came into focus.

His gaze landed on my Kindle. "Were you up late reading again?" He narrowed his eyes.

"There was never a good stopping place." I bristled defensively.

Dad shook his head. "Well, I guess it could be worse."

"A lot worse," I reminded him, shoving off my covers. "You would die if you knew what other kids my age were doing at night."

His eyes widened. "I don't want to know."

"You're right." I stood up, teetering precariously on my swollen ankle. Leaning over, I pressed a kiss to his cheek. "You don't."

A worried look crossed Dad's face as he glanced down at my ankle. "Still hurting today?"

I waved away his concern. "It's fine. Just a sprain. It'll be better soon."

"Are you sure? I can stay home and take you to the doctor if you need."

"I can walk on it. See." I took a few wobbly steps. "I don't need to see a doctor."

"You've always been stubborn," Dad said, his lips curling at the edges. "Try to stay awake during class, okay?"

I shook my head. "I'll do my best."

"Skyler's giving you a ride to school, right?" Dad asked.

"Yep." Dad made me text her last night to ask for a ride. I hated doing it, but I knew if I didn't Dad would insist on taking me, and I didn't want him to go into work late.

"Good. I'm heading to work. See you tonight."

"Yeah, see ya," I called as he walked down the hallway. After opening my dresser drawer, I perused it for something to wear. My fingers fanned over t-shirts and jeans in search of something. Usually I grabbed the first thing I saw and threw it on. *What was my problem today?*

Cooper's face filled my mind, his blue eyes and dimpled smile. Chills skated up my spine remembering how it felt with his arms around me. I conjured up the memory of the way he smelled, of his kind eyes and caring demeanor. Chastising myself, I picked out a pair of jeans and a t-shirt. Then I stalked across the hall to the bathroom. After stepping into the shower, I snatched up the soap and scrubbed my skin hard, hoping it could erase all traces of Cooper from my mind. The last thing I needed was to get all tangled up about Cooper Montgomery. Sure he was nice yesterday, but it meant nothing. I would've bet anything that at school today he'd completely ignore me. He would be too busy with with popular, gorgeous girls like Calista, girls who fit the mold. I was not that girl, and I never would be.

Besides, I shouldn't want his attention. I'd already made a mistake I vowed I never would. Allowing Cooper into my home, especially when Dad wasn't here, was stupid. No, it was beyond stupid. It was irresponsible. And it wouldn't happen again. I wouldn't have another error in judgment. Never again would I allow Cooper's dimples and blue eyes to sway me. I'd stay strong. Strong like stones, like bricks, like nails.

Since I woke up late and then spent way too much time daydreaming, I didn't have time to blow-dry my hair. Instead, I pulled it back into a bun at the nape of my neck. A few wet strands fell out while I limped over to Skyler's house. I tucked them behind my ear before rapping on Skyler's front door.

When she answered it, her black hair hung smoothly down her back, her eyelids shimmered, her eyelashes long and curled. For having to get up so early, she looked really nice. She'd been able to pull it together a lot better than I had, and I always got up this early.

"Hey, I'm sorry about this," I told her.

"No problem." She looked at my foot. "I couldn't let you ride your bike with a sprained ankle."

"What are you going to do during zero period?"

"Hang in the library." She walked past me, making her way over to her little red Toyota. "Don't worry about me."

Skyler used her usual speedy gait, her long legs moving swiftly and gracefully. I, on the other hand, resembled one of the Walking Dead. By the time I hobbled over to the car, she was already inside gliding on pink lip gloss while studying her reflection in the rearview mirror. When I slid into the passenger seat, she tossed the lip gloss to me. "Here. You could use some."

Catching me off guard, I barely had time to react. However, my reflexes kicked in and I caught it. "I'm good."

"C'mon, put a little on. It won't bite." She turned on the engine and pulled away from the curb.

I stared at the lip gloss in my palm. Lifting my head, I caught my reflection in the side mirror. My skin was even more pale than usual. Maybe a little color would help. Shrugging, I smoothed a little gloss on my lips and then rubbed them together.

"So, you gonna tell me about Cooper or do I have to beg?" Skyler asked, as she turned the steering wheel, the car turning the corner.

She must've seen Cooper at my house. My face flamed. "There's nothing to tell."

Her head whipped around, her mouth falling open. "Nothing to tell? He was at your house!" She was doing that squealing thing she did when she got overly excited.

I cringed, kind of wishing I had ear plugs. "Remember I fell off my bike?" I pointed to my ankle. "Cooper happened to be driving by, and he stopped to help me."

"Oh, how romantic." Skyler clutched her chest, her eyes taking on a dreamy quality.

"It is not romantic," I said. "It meant nothing."

Skyler gave me a smug smile. "If he was only helping you get home, why did he stay so long?"

"Damn, you're nosy," I teased her.

"I wouldn't have to be if you didn't always hold out on me." She winked.

"Yeah, because my life is full of secrets and

intrigue."

"Maybe not before, but now it seems like it is." She nudged me in the side with her free arm. "C'mon. You spent the afternoon with Cooper Montgomery while I was at home helping Mom make a batch of tortillas and listening to my brothers play videogames. The least you could do is fill me in on the details."

I chuckled at the picture she'd drawn. I'd often told her she could write a story. "Fine. He came over and iced my ankle."

Skyler sighed, that weird wistful look on her face again. The school came into view, and I was grateful. Only another minute and then I could get out of this car, effectively ending this conversation.

"Then he asked why I was out riding my bike wearing my backpack, and I told him that I was on the way to the library to type up my article on him."

"Why didn't you come over to my house?" Skyler pulled into the school parking lot. It was practically empty with a few cars scattered here and there. By the time first period started, the whole lot would be crammed, but during zero period it was like a ghost town.

"I didn't want to bother you," I lied.

"You're never a bother." She smiled. "I would've welcomed the distraction from my family."

I grinned, knowing she was right. "Anyway, he loaned me his laptop so I could type the article."

"Shut up!" She said emphatically, slapping me in the shoulder.

"I wish you'd let me," I mumbled.

She giggled. "You know what I mean."

I nodded. *Yeah, I did.* She was surprised, and I totally got that. I had been a little shocked by his kind gesture too.

After Skyler parked, I yanked up my backpack and struggled to get out of the car. I was not looking forward to limping around campus all day. There was no way to go undetected with my ankle like this. Kids would notice, and that was something I dreaded.

"Sounds like he's totally into you." Skyler came around the car to meet me.

"He is not." My chest tightened at her words. I knew she wasn't correct, but there was a part of me that wanted so desperately to believe it. To grasp the words and hold them close, as if by doing so they would come true. But life wasn't like that. I had learned that the hard way. Wanting something didn't make it real. Wishes were nothing but unanswered prayers, fleeting thoughts we never saw come to fruition. They scarred you if you allowed them to, if you foolishly put your hopes in them.

And that was something I wouldn't do again.

CHAPTER 10
Cooper

I never made it to Calista's last night. A fact which she couldn't stop reminding me of today. Frankly, it was starting to piss me off. And it was the reason why I didn't get involved in relationships. Once that happened, the girl became needy and suddenly demanded all my time and attention. I was a busy guy. I couldn't spend all my time with some girl. Besides, I had baseball and school, and that required my focus right now. If I had any hope of getting into a good college, I couldn't allow some chick to take over my life.

"I waited for you for hours." Calista leaned her back against my locker, sticking her bottom lip out in a pout. It was sexy as hell, but it didn't quell my irritation.

"Look, I told you, something came up, okay?"

"Hey, Coop," Nate waved from his locker across the hall. When I lifted my hand to wave back, his gaze shifted to Calista, and he cocked an eyebrow.

I flashed him a knowing smile.

"What came up that was so important?" Calista asked, yanking my attention back to her. One thing that was clear was that she liked to be the center of attention. God, she was exhausting.

London floated into my mind. I remembered

how helpless she appeared lying on the ground, blood on her hands. And then I recalled her open expression filled with sorrow when she told me about her mom. I knew that pain, and in that instant I felt connected to her. Felt like she was the one person on earth who understood me.

"Cooper? Where were you last night?" Calista pressed.

There was no way I would tell her about being at London's house. I didn't plan on telling anyone. Besides, it didn't matter. It's not like I was planning to hang out with her again. We may have had one moment of connection, but it didn't mean anything. When it passed, it was clear that she wanted me to leave as much as I wanted to get out of there. We weren't compatible. We were total opposites. Plus, I wasn't kidding when I said she had a major chip on her shoulder. She was like ice, she was so frigid. Anytime she started to thaw, to reveal a part of herself, she quickly closed back up, freezing me out. If I thought Calista was high maintenance, London was ten times worse. At least with Calista I knew what I was getting.

"Nothing. It was just a--" Clattering caught my attention. I turned my head in time to see London stumble over in the middle of the hallway. Maybe her ankle was worse than I thought.

A laugh bubbled from Calista's throat. "What a loser."

When I scanned the hallway, everyone was chuckling, pointing and whispering, but not one person was helping her. London placed her palms on the ground and pushed herself up. She held her head high, but I could see the struggle on her face as she fought against the embarrassment. Before I knew it, I was in front of her, holding out my hand. It's like my body had a mind of its own, as if I couldn't control it.

London looked as stunned as I felt when she peered up at me. But she took my hand in hers. When I closed my fingers around her palm, I smiled. "We have to stop meeting like this."

She smiled wanly as I tugged on her arm. "I lost my balance." Once she was upright, I released her hand and she looked downward. "Damn ankle."

"That's right. Let him have it."

Her eyes found mine, and her lips curved upward. "Thanks for helping me." She paused, her eyelashes fluttering. Normally when girls did that it was meant to be flirty, but I could tell that wasn't her intention. Yet her innocence made it seem even more seductive. "Again."

"Any time," I said, and then quickly amended. "With your track record, maybe it was a mistake to say that."

A small giggle escaped through her lips. She didn't appear to laugh often, and it gave me a strange sense of satisfaction to know that I had elicited it. "Don't worry. I'll try to keep the accidents to a minimum as much as possible."

"That would probably be a good thing," I said.

"Well, I better get to class." She cast her gaze downward.

"Do you need help?" I asked, and then immediately regretted it. When my gaze swept the halls, I saw the horrified stares from Nate and a few of the other guys. I hadn't even thought about them when I came rushing over here like a damn knight in shining armor. Swallowing hard, I craned my neck in Calista's direction. If I thought my friend's faces were bad, they were nothing compared to Calista's. She was practically shooting daggers at me with her eyes.

"I'm fine," London said swiftly, and then hobbled around me.

I was ashamed at how relieved I was that she didn't take me up on my offer. What was wrong with me? My emotions were so conflicted when I was around her. No one else had ever had this effect on me before.

"What was that about?" Calista sidled up next to me.

"She fell, and I helped her."

"Why?"

My previous embarrassment turned to disgust. "The better question is, why didn't you? Why didn't anyone?" Running a hand over my head, I spun around and stormed away. I didn't even stop when Nate called my name. Honestly, I was disgusted with all of them.

London was up ahead, limping slowly. She hadn't made it very far, and it was clear she wouldn't make it anywhere very fast. It only took a second to catch up to her.

"I gotta be honest, you don't seem fine," I said, grinning.

"I look that bad, huh?" She wrinkled her button nose.

With her hair pulled back and no glasses on, her eyes appeared even wider than usual, the unique color even more striking. Her lips held a hint of shimmer, her skin was so pale it resembled snow.

"No, you don't," I breathed out the words.

She bit her lip. I hardly knew her and already I knew she did this when she felt nervous. Kids flew past us, all hurrying to class, but we were moving at a snail's pace. I found myself wanting to put my arms around London and guide her to class. But I couldn't do that. Not here. Besides, from the little I knew of her, I didn't think she'd welcome it anyway.

"At least let me hold your bag," I offered.

She hesitated. Then a slow smile crept across her face. "Okay."

I carefully removed her backpack and held it in my fingers. My arm lowered from the weight of it. "Damn, what do you have in here?"

"Books. What else?" She took a step forward, dragging her maimed foot.

"You know we have lockers for a reason, right?"

Darkness fell like a curtain over her eyes, but she recovered quickly. "Oh, is that what they're for? For our books? I'll have to try that out sometime."

There was more to this, but I didn't want to pry. It wasn't my business. I was merely helping her to class. "Where are we headed?"

"Mr. Humphrey's."

"Ah, I'm sorry." I nodded knowingly, and she chuckled. Mr. Humphrey was known for being a hard ass. Plus, he taught math, so it was bad on all counts.

"He's all right." She shrugged. We neared the classroom. A few more students passed us, vanishing into the classrooms lining the walls. One of the girls bumped into London and she teetered on the balls of her feet. Reaching out my arm, I steadied her. She wore a sheepish expression. "The teachers I can handle."

I swiveled my head in the direction of the girl who bumped London. That's when I recognized her as one of Calista's friends. She flashed London a smug look before disappearing around the corner. Clearly the bump wasn't an accident. It made me wonder if London's locker aversion had anything to do with bullying, and that thought turned my stomach. It's not that I didn't know bullying took place. I guess it was something I didn't think much about. My focus was always on my schoolwork and baseball. Everything else had become white noise.

"Thanks for walking me to class." London reached for her backpack, plucking it from my fingers. Then she flung it over her shoulder.

"Hey," I stopped her before she could turn around. "I read the article. It was really good." I was surprised that she hadn't mentioned my grandparents or Calista. She could've really smeared me or delved into my personal life, but she didn't. She stuck to baseball and the facts like a real reporter, like a professional. Obviously she took writing seriously, the same way I took baseball. It seemed I was always finding similarities between the two of us.

"Thanks." She smiled. "I hope John likes it. I haven't heard from him yet."

"I'm sure he will."

"If so, it will come out in next week's edition." The bell pealed, and her eyes widened. "Thanks again. I have to go."

While she slipped into Mr. Humphrey's classroom, I hurried down the hallway toward my science class, cursing myself for spending so much time talking to London. I'd never been late to class before. *What the hell had gotten into me today?*

"So what's the deal with you and the newspaper chick?" Nate asked while we walked toward the bus carrying our team to the away game.

"Nothing." I shifted the bag on my shoulder.

"Rumor is that you flaked on Calista to go to newspaper chick's house," Nate continued.

My body went hot, and I glanced around to see if anyone else was listening in. Brandon and Alec were the closest to us, but they were too busy laughing at something on Alec's phone. Who had told people about me being at London's? The memory flickered of the dark haired girl from next door. She looked familiar. I was sure she went to school here. Had she told people? I had a feeling London would be as unhappy about this as I was.

"Is it true, man?" Nate asked.

We reached the bus and I climbed up the steps. "Yeah, but it's not what you're thinking. Trust me."

"Hey, it's not me you've gotta convince."

As if on cue, my phone buzzed in my pocket. Stomach sinking, I dug it out.

Calista: Now I know what your big

"emergency" was.

Shaking my head, I shoved the phone back into my pocket. That was it. I'd been nice to Calista long enough. That chick had to go.

"She's pretty upset, dude," Nate said.

"I don't care," I said harshly, finding an empty seat and dropping into it. "It's not like she's my girlfriend. We hooked up once."

"Hey, I get it, man." Nate slid in next to me. "Really I do. But you know Calista. She's pissed, and when she gets pissed, she gets even."

"What are you saying?" Dread sank into my gut.

"I'm saying that if you're not into newspaper chick, you better make sure Calista knows it or else Calista's going to make the girl's life a living hell."

Shit. I knew hooking up with Calista was a mistake.

CHAPTER 11
London

Annabelle returned on Thursday, just in time to help us read through the newspaper one last time before Mr. Smith submitted it to the printers. John was our editor, so technically he ran the Gold Rush Gazette, but he was a student like the rest of us. Therefore, Mr. Smith was the ultimate authority. He oversaw the paper and made sure what we printed was appropriate. Basically, it was his head on the chopping block if we wrote something we shouldn't.

Annabelle and I had never been friends, and it was pretty evident that we never would be. She acted like I stole her article right from under her. As if that had been my plan all along. No matter how hard I tried to convince her otherwise, she remained pissed off.

And I wasn't in the mood. It was late, and I was tired. All I wanted to do was go home and curl up with a good book. Instead, I was sitting in a plastic chair in the middle of a cramped classroom staring at a tiny computer screen. Editing was my least favorite part of the writing process, and Annabelle was making it even worse.

When I wouldn't engage with Annabelle, she finally unleashed on John. "You couldn't have pushed back Cooper's article another week?"

John ran an agitated hand over his sandy

brown hair. "C'mon, Annabelle. You know our next issue doesn't come out for six more weeks. By that time the fall baseball season would be almost over. The article needed to come out at the beginning of the season, not the end." He snorted. "If we did that we might as well wait until the spring season to write the article."

Huffing, she crossed her arms over her chest. He was right, and she knew it. I bit back a smug smile as she pressed her lips together, unable to come up with an argument. She'd already tried to bring Mr. Smith into it, but he deferred to John, so there wasn't anything else for Annabelle to do. Leaning back in my chair, I bit the cap of my pen and read over the article on the screen. The scent of sweat, pencil shavings and whiteboard markers filled my senses.

Realizing she had no other recourse, Annabelle finally flung herself into a nearby chair with a resigned sigh. The remainder of the staff worked on their respective assignments, and an hour later all the articles had been read, edited, and approved. Standing up, I stretched my arms up high above my head. A yawn escaped through my lips, and I rolled my kinked neck.

Pulling out my phone, I shot off a text to my dad to see when he could pick me up. I had ridden to school with Skyler again, but I didn't want to bother her to come back and pick me up. Man, I would be happy when my ankle was completely healed. It was feeling a little better today. I was able to put pressure on it and walk with more stability, so I was sure it would be better soon. By the time the response from Dad came the rest of the staff had left and it was only John, me, and Mr. Smith.

Dad: Sorry, pumpkin. Still working. Will be there in 1 hr.

I blew out a frustrated breath and shoved my phone into my pocket.

"Need a ride home?" John asked.

Sometimes John was annoying, but most of the time he was a nice enough guy. And we'd worked together on the paper for two years now. Still the idea of him driving me home made my skin crawl. The familiar prickle of fear tingled up my spine. "No, it's okay." After snatching my backpack off the floor, I slung it over my shoulder.

"You sure?" He pressed.

I nodded. "Yeah, my dad's coming to get me."

"All right." John turned off the computer nearest to him, and then picked up his book bag.

"See you later, John," I called as I stepped out of the classroom. "Bye Mr. Smith."

"See ya," John responded. Mr. Smith waved from his desk, the light glinting off his glasses.

It was darker than I thought it would be when I walked outside, and I shivered. I stared out at the street, wondering what I would do to kill time until Dad arrived. My homework called from my backpack, and I scoured the area looking for a place with some light where I could sit down. A few feet away was a bench with a streetlamp above it. As I made my way over to it, movement and noise caught my attention. My head bobbed up, my eyes landing on the baseball field. It was lit up, the team out on the field. From where I stood, I spotted Cooper on the mound.

Abandoning thoughts of studying, I moved toward the field. It was a long trek across the grass, and I was grateful that my ankle was healing. Last time I'd been out here was for Cooper's game. I'd never been here during nighttime. It seemed almost magical with the bright lights shining over the green grass and yellow sand of the field. By the time I reached it, the team was dispersing. Some were grabbing their bags, while others were already heading out to the parking lot.

My gaze swept the field and dugout searching for Cooper, but he was nowhere in sight. I was about ready to turn around when I heard his voice. It was coming from somewhere behind the bleachers. I crept forward, running my fingers along the cold metal until I finally reached the other side. Cooper's back was to me when I approached.

"Damn it." He threw his glove on the ground and it landed with a thud in the thick green reeds. He tore off his ball cap, causing his hair to stick up in spikes all over his head. The muscles on his arm bulged as he fisted the hat in his hands, squeezing as if it was a stress ball.

Feeling like I was infringing on a private moment, I turned around. Only I misjudged how close the bleachers were to me, and rammed my knee into the corner.

"Shit," I cursed under my breath.

"London?"

Double shit.

Rubbing my knee through my jeans, I whirled around.

"What are you doing here?"

Not exactly a warm welcome, but then again what did I expect when I snuck up on him like this. "Um…I…I'm sorry. I um…was working on the paper, and now I needed to kill time until Dad comes to get me."

"Kill time, huh?" One side of his mouth curved upward. "So what you're telling me is that you planned to use me?"

I giggled, grateful for the shift in his mood. "Yes, I guess I did."

"I suppose I should respect your honesty. Most people won't admit to that right off the bat."

"I'm not most people," I said, surprised by my own boldness. Something about Cooper made me more confident. It was weird.

"No, you're not." He glanced down at my foot. "Your ankle seems to be getting better."

"Yeah," I agreed. "It's healing nicely."

For a moment he studied me, then his expression grew somber. "Hey, I'm sorry about earlier. How much of my tantrum did you see?"

"Not much," I said. "What happened?"

"Just had a really shitty practice." He dropped his hat on the ground near his feet and ran a hand through his hair. A few of the unruly strands smoothed back out.

I shrugged. "At least it was only a practice."

"I wish that was the case, but I played so poorly in our game last night the coach had to pull me in the second inning." His jaw tensed, his hands fisting at his sides. "I can't afford to screw up like this. Not now. Not this year."

The desperation in his voice cut to my heart. I paused, choosing my words carefully. "I totally get why you're so upset. But when I saw you play, you were incredible. One game can't take that away. And I'm sure you'll get it together in time for Monday's game."

His eyes narrowed, his head cocking to the side. My stomach dropped, worried that I'd said the wrong thing. "You know our schedule?"

I mentally chastised myself. God, I probably sounded like a damn stalker to him. "Yeah, I memorized it as part of my research for the article." My face heated up. "I know it sounds silly, but I get really into my articles. I get that it's a stupid school newspaper to everyone else, but it means something to me." Why, oh why was I still rambling? I was sure he didn't care about any of this. In fact, I was fairly certain it made me sound even more idiotic.

"I get it." He nodded. "I sometimes feel like that with baseball. To most of the guys on the team, baseball is a hobby. After high school they might play recreationally, or maybe they'll stop playing altogether. But with me, it's different. I plan to play professionally, and I know I'll never be able to quit."

His words pierced my heart, snaking their way inside and squeezing hard. He *did* understand. He was the first person who ever had. And I wasn't sure how I felt about that.

"London." Cooper stepped toward me, causing my pulse to quicken. His eyes seared into mine, and I swallowed hard.

"Cooper?"

I flinched at the sound of Calista's voice. She

stepped around the bleachers, Cooper's hat perched on top of her blond curls. Her presence reminded me what a fool I was being. I never should have come over here. It would have been smarter to stay in front of the school, studying. What had I been thinking? That was the problem. I didn't think when it came to Cooper. His dimpled smile and blue eyes had cast a spell on me, and I seemed to lose my brain around him.

"What's she doing here?" Calista glared at me. "I thought you two were done with the article."

I opened my mouth to explain, but Cooper spoke before I could. "It's none of your business what we're doing, Calista."

She reeled back from his words. "W-what?"

"You and I fooled around one time, and that was it," he said coldly. "You're not my girlfriend, and I don't owe you any explanations."

Calista's face fell. A part of me felt a sick sense of satisfaction by it, but the other part felt badly for her. Clearly what happened between them meant something to her, and she'd misinterpreted his feelings. But I didn't feel like it was her fault. I felt like it was his. And I realized that what happened to Calista could easily have happened to me. Hadn't I, too, been sucked in by Cooper's charm? Maybe this was his game, to draw you in and spit you out.

"Fine. You can have your damn hat back then." Calista yanked the hat off her head and threw it at him. Then she spun around and stalked off, her hair frizzy and piled high on her head.

"Sorry about that," Cooper said when she was out of earshot.

"So am I," I took a step backward. "See ya around, Cooper."

"Wait." He stopped me. "Are you upset with me?"

"Boy, you sure are perceptive." I let out a bitter laugh.

His gaze slid over my shoulder, then back to my face. His eyebrows knit together in a pensive expression. "Let me get this straight. You're mad because of how I treated Calista?"

I nodded.

"But I've seen the way she treats you. It's horrible."

"True, but that still doesn't justify what you did. You used her, and you should be ashamed of yourself." With a shake of my head, I pivoted on my heels and made my way across the field. I didn't bother looking back as I headed toward the front of the school. When I reached it, I wondered why I hadn't stayed here to begin with. Before Calista had walked up the connection to Cooper was so thick I could feel it, and it reminded me of when he was at my house. I didn't normally feel that way with people, and a part of me wanted desperately to hold on to it. But I couldn't ignore what he'd done to Calista. He may have seemed like a nice guy, but he was a charmer and a player. He hooked up with girls and dumped them like they were trash. And I couldn't let him treat me like that. I wouldn't be another girl to add to his list.

In the short time I'd known Cooper, one thing had become painfully clear. If I fell for him, he'd break my heart, and I'd be powerless to stop it.

CHAPTER 12
Cooper

It had been a shitty week. Baseball sucked, and girls confused the hell out of me. That's how I found myself at a party on Friday night with Nate. He didn't even have to beg me this time. I was game the second he sent the text. To say that he was surprised would be an understatement, especially since it was at Calista's house. The parties often were at her house, because her parents were out of town so frequently and she had two college-aged brothers who could buy booze.

Calista didn't worry me. I was sure she'd moved on by now. She wasn't one to sit around and lick her wounds. Lick some other guy's face was more like it.

All I wanted was one night where I didn't have to overthink everything, where I didn't have to worry. For some reason I couldn't get London out of my thoughts. The look she gave me when she stormed off was permanently etched in my mind like a goddamn tattoo. She was impossible to decipher. I had helped her when she fell off her bike, practically nursed her ankle back to health, walked her to class and carried her backpack, even at the risk of ridicule. Then, to top it all off, I stuck up for her with Calista. And yet, she acted like I was the bad guy. Like I was the jerk. Maybe she should look in a freaking mirror.

Normally when I went to parties I was the DD since I didn't like to drink anyway. I hated not having complete control. But this week I wanted to lose control, to be numb. So Troy, our second baseman, drove us. No way would Nate offer to be DD. He had absolutely no self-control around alcohol. He was like a goddamn kid in a candy store when we were surrounded by booze. That was another reason I generally didn't like to party with him.

"You have to keep me away from the girls," I told Nate on the way to the party. We sat in the backseat, Troy and Brandon were up front.

"No way. I don't want that responsibility. Now that you're not tied to Calista, girls will be all over you," Nate said.

I bristled at his statement. "I was never tied to Calista."

"That's not what she told people."

"Damn it." I ground my teeth. "This is exactly why I need to stay away from girls. I'm done with chicks, man."

"Dude, you better not be turning gay, because I'm so not into that shit."

I chuckled. "Don't worry, you're not my type."

Nate smiled. "Are you shitting me? I'm everyone's type."

"You wish." I glanced out the window as Troy turned the corner. We were on Calista's street, nearing her house. Cars lined the curb. *Subtle.* "I'm sure no one knows Calista's having a party," I said sarcastically, my stomach tightening. All it would take was one neighbor calling the cops for my life to unravel. Maybe this was a bad idea.

"Don't sweat it." Nate clamped a hand on my shoulder. "Everything's going to be fine."

Famous last words. Still, I had no choice at this point, so when Troy cut the engine, I hopped out of the car. Cool air circled me, the scent of damp earth and grass wafting under my nose. The sound of music and chatter rose from the house and swelled around us. Nervous, I glanced at the quiet suburban street, at the row of two-story houses, yellow light shining from the windows. Troy and Brandon were already heading inside when Nate and I started walking up the stairs to the front porch.

There were even more people here than last time. Calista sure knew how to draw a crowd, I'd give her that. I noticed a few college-aged guys scattered around. One of them I recognized as Calista's brother, Rhett, and my chest tightened, wondering what she'd told him about me. But when he smiled and threw me a wave, my shoulders relaxed.

"Beers are in the kitchen." Brandon hopped in front of us, already holding a bottle in his hand.

"Thanks, man." Nate slapped him on the back before making a beeline for the kitchen. A few guys were pulling beers out of a cooler sitting on the tile floor. Nate grabbed two out, reached for the bottle opener on the counter and popped off the caps. Then he handed me one.

When I folded my hand around the glass bottle it was cold, and liquid coated my palm. Leaning my back against the wall, I scoured the room. Girls holding red plastic cups stood around in clusters chatting and laughing. One of them peered over in my direction and smiled. Without thinking, I grinned back.

"Oh, no you don't." Nate tugged on my arm.

Remembering our earlier conversation, I chuckled and allowed him to pull me into the living room. Not that it was much help. There were hot girls sprinkled all around this room too. A tanned blond caught my eye, throwing me a wink.

"Shit, man, we haven't even been here two minutes and already you've got them honing in on you. It's like you're wearing a goddamn target or something." Zach's eyes widened. "Or a tracking device. They can sense you coming."

I took a sip of my beer. The bitter taste slid over my tongue and down my throat. "You're crazy."

A brunette wearing a shirt that barely covered her chest and shorts that stopped just under her ass swaggered over to us. But this time it wasn't me she had her sights set on.

"Hey," she said, her eyes locking with Nate. "I've seen you around. Nate, right?"

"That's me. And what's your name, beautiful?"

She giggled, twirling her hair around her index finger. "Heather."

"Nice." Nate nodded in appreciation, his gaze roving over Heather's body. Then he leaned over and whispered, "Sorry, bro. You're on your own."

I shoved him away, knowing this was inevitable. "Go. Have fun." As if he really needed my permission. He barely even waited for me to finish my sentence before he was heading off with Heather. Taking another sip of my beer, I walked further into the living room searching for Brandon or Troy. My feet tapped on the hardwood floor and I passed large framed paintings hanging on the wall. I noticed a few other guys from the team were seated on a leather couch in front of a large window sipping beers and talking. One of them looked up in my direction.

"Hey, Coop." He nodded.

"Hey, man," I responded and stepped forward, intending to walk over to him.

"Oh, look what the cat dragged in." Calista's voice stopped me.

I turned around wearing a smile. "No cat. It was Nate who invited me."

By the hard expression on her face, I was guessing my little joke didn't work on her. Instead, she pursed her lips, crossing her arms over her chest. "Did you bring *her* with you?"

"Who?"

"That loser you can't seem to stay away from."

I cringed at the word "loser." Gritting my teeth, I said, "Her name's London."

"Whatever." She shrugged.

"And no, she's not with me." Lifting the beer to my lips, I took a long swallow. In a minute I planned to search for something stronger. I wondered what was in the red cups. The blond that had been eyeing me earlier sauntered over, her lips stretching into a broad smile.

"Hey, baby," I drawled, more for Calista's

90

benefit than anything. Perhaps now she'd leave me the hell alone.

"Oh, don't bother with him," Calista said. "You're not his type. He likes girls who wear glasses and thrift store clothes, and walk around with their nose stuck in a book." A confused look passed over the blond's delicate features.

"Ignore her," I said to the blond.

Calista glared at me. "Actually, it's a good thing you didn't bring nerdgirl here. She'd probably have no idea how to behave in a neighborhood like ours. It's a little too rich for her blood, I think."

London's words floated through my mind. *You used her, and you should be ashamed.* Calista had done nothing but treat London like shit, and yet London still defended her. She believed that Calista deserved respect. But she was wrong. Calista didn't deserve it at all. London may have walked around like she was an ice queen, but inside her heart was warm and kind. The same couldn't be said of Calista.

"I think you've just proved that having money doesn't make you classy," I said to Calista.

In response, she swallowed hard, her chest heaving with each labored breath.

Taking a sip of my beer, I turned to the blond girl. "Don't listen to her. She's just jealous, and she has absolutely no clue what the hell she's talking about. Wanna go somewhere more private?" Snaking my arm around the girl's waist, I guided her into the adjoining room. She leaned into me, her hair sliding over my shoulder. It smelled like peaches. When we found an empty corner, I rested my back against the wall and grinned at the blond. Warning bells went off

91

in my mind, remembering my plea to Nate about keeping me away from girls. The last thing I needed right now was another cling-on like Calista, or a puzzle I couldn't figure out like London.

Pushing both of them from my mind, I winked at the pretty blond wearing an impossibly short jean skirt and skintight top that left nothing to the imagination. "So, what's your name?"

"Emma," she said.

"Nice to meet you, Emma. I'm--"

"I know who you are, Cooper Montgomery," she interrupted.

"So, you're a baseball fan?"

She reached out her hands, splaying them on my chest. Her fingers danced over my muscles. "I'm a fan of yours. Does that count?"

"Yeah. That definitely counts." After taking the last swig of my beer, I set it down on a nearby table and took the blond girl in my arms. Maybe I didn't need to get drunk tonight. Perhaps I could lose myself in Emma. And that would be it. I would make it clear that we were nothing more than a one-night thing. No giving her my hat, or number, or anything. After my internal pep-talk, I lowered my head, capturing her lips in mine. Her lip gloss tasted like cherries, and my heart picked up speed. Raking my hands up her back, I tangled my fingers in her long hair, pulling gently. A tiny sound of pleasure emitted from the back of Emma's throat. *Oh, yeah, she would be too easy.* I slid my tongue into her mouth, swirling it inside. She reached under my shirt, and her hands felt good against my bare skin. She was eager, her lips moving swiftly, her hands exploring my chest. Maybe too eager. And it made me feel like shit.

I'd made out with tons of girls, hooked up with a lot of them too. And I never felt guilty. I figured they wanted it as much as I did. But now I wasn't so sure. Was a one-night thing really enough for them? It hadn't been for Calista. She'd wanted more, and when I couldn't give it to her, she'd turned into a royal pain in my ass.

When I drew back, Emma's eyes were half-lidded. She had that satisfied yet hungry look on her face. Lip gloss smeared her cheek, and her hair was messy. She slid her hands up to my shoulders and tugged me close, pressing her chest to mine. Biting her lip, she leaned into me, her face nearing mine again. An image of London standing in front of me chewing on her lower lip crashed into me with such force, I pulled away from Emma. She raised one eyebrow, a silent question.

I hooked up with girls all the time and never called them again, but in my mind there wasn't anything wrong with that. All the guys did it. But now I couldn't get London's words out of my head. Was she right? Was I hurting these girls?

God, I hated that her words had gotten to me like this. Why did I even care what she thought?

When Emma's lips covered mine again, I responded, my mouth moving in sync with hers. Why was I even thinking about London right now? I had an incredibly hot girl practically begging for it. *What the hell was wrong with me?*

Calista's voice reached my ears from across the room. I peeked out of one eye and saw her talking to a friend. But then she glanced in my direction. I saw the hurt in her eyes the second before she averted her gaze. Damn, I had treated her pretty shitty. She always wore this hard exterior, but she was a person underneath it all.

I'd never been outright mean to a girl like that. What had made me do it?

The words "loser" and "nerdgirl" floated through my mind. It was because she'd put down London. The anger I felt toward her wasn't about me, it was about London. Detaching my lips from Emma's, I took a deep breath, the revelation making me dizzy.

What was it about London that brought out this hero side of me? And more importantly, why the hell couldn't I get her off my mind?

CHAPTER 13
London

On Monday the Gold Rush Gazette came out. It was always exciting for me when an edition of the paper circulated. I knew the rest of the school didn't give a rat's ass. The teachers passed them out in homeroom, and by second period I would find them littering the school hallways and trash bins. The faculty had been trying to talk Mr. Smith into making the editions paperless for the past couple of years. We'd fought them on it, and so far we'd won. But every time I saw the papers strewn around campus I knew we'd end up losing at some point. The thought of our paper only being available online worried me. I liked the feeling of the paper in my hands, I liked seeing Dad tack it to the fridge. But mostly, I knew that once it was online no one would ever read it. I suspected there were some students who read it for no other reason than that we passed it out and they were bored. But if they had to go on the website on their own time that would never happen.

Before leaving homeroom, I picked up a couple extra copies to bring home. Pressing them to my chest, I stepped out of the classroom. I was no longer limping today. In fact, I'd ridden my bike this morning. My ankle still hurt a little, but nothing I couldn't handle. The hallway was filled with students. Chatter and laughter encompassed me, the scent of deodorant, hairspray and perfume overwhelming. My skin crawled as I pushed past backpacks, elbows, and flailing arms. I was not fond of crowds. When I graduated sixth grade, Dad thought a trip to Disneyland would be a fun reward. And it should have been. Most kid love Disneyland. I mean, it's the happiest place on earth, right? But for me, it wasn't. I spent two grueling days fighting off panic attacks and fear. There was nowhere I could go to get away from the crowds of people. We actually had a three-day pass, but we left before the third day. And I was grateful. I wasn't sure I'd survive it any longer. Even now when I thought about it, my pulse spiked, and breathing became difficult.

A shoulder rammed into mine, my skin smarting. Reaching down, I rubbed my hand over it. But then I got slammed from the other side. *What the hell?* Losing my grip on the newspapers, I opened up my fingers and they slid from my hands, fluttering to the floor, graceful like birds. They landed flat out, the article about Cooper staring up at me. His smile and bright eyes mocked me from where the picture lie on the scuffed linoleum.

"Oops, sorry." I recognized Calista's voice immediately. "Here. Let me help you." She bent over to pick up the papers off the ground.

I stood frozen, surprised by her offer. When I glanced around the hallway I saw others looking on curiously. A funny feeling descended in the pit of my stomach. What was she up to? She wore a sweet smile when she stood, thrusting the papers toward me. Tentatively, I clamped my fingers around them. A hand touched my back, and I flinched.

"Oh, so jumpy." Calista said, her hand resting on my back.

Wriggling, I moved away from her. A clicking sound caught my attention. "What was that?" I whipped around. A few of her friends stood just feet away, guilty expressions cloaking their faces. Calista giggled.

Now I knew something was going on. Biting my lip, I gripped tightly to the newspaper, my gaze shifting around the hallway.

Before walking away, Calista leaned in close and whispered in my ear, "It was a valiant effort, but you had to know you couldn't keep a guy like Cooper interested in a girl like you for very long." She winked. "He was at my house on Friday night, and from what I could see he wasn't thinking about you at all."

My heart pounded in my chest when she stalked off with her friends, her laughter trailing behind her like a kite. Had Cooper really been with her on Friday night? It seemed so odd after the way he'd treated her on Thursday. Then again, it confirmed my suspicions about him. Hadn't I pegged him as a charmer and a user? No matter how kind and genuine he acted, I had seen right through him.

And it wasn't like we were friends or anything. We talked a couple of times. That was it. Nothing more. Nothing less. And now that the article was out and my ankle was healed, we'd never have to talk again. Sadness swept over me at the thought, but I shook it away.

Swallowing hard, I held my head high and took deliberate steps to class. By the time I reached it, the ink from the paper had seeped into the moist skin of my palms. My nerves rattled when I walked into the classroom and found my seat. After peeling the papers from my hands, I set them on the desk, dropped my backpack on the floor and sat down. Black ink dotted my skin, so I wiped my palms on my jeans.

Low giggles erupted behind me and then rolled through the room, like waves in the ocean. The sound would crescendo and then die down, only to peak again a second later. When I turned to see what was funny, all eyes were turned to me. Frantically, I glanced down at my clothes and hands. Had I gotten ink all over myself? But I didn't see anything out of the ordinary, just a couple black spots from where I wiped my hands. *Uh-oh.* Did I touch my face?

The bell rang and Mrs. Henley stood from her desk. The giggling died down a little, but I could still hear it. It burned my ears and poisoned my thoughts. Reaching in my pocket, I tugged out my phone. After turning on the camera, I pressed the button so it would face me as if I was going to take a selfie, which I wasn't. Definitely not. I had no idea how to take a decent one. Skyler had perfected the art of the selfie, able to capture shots of herself that looked like they belonged in a magazine. The few times I'd tried, I resembled Jabba the Hutt, complete with neck rolls and a double chin. It was strange because I didn't even have those in real life. *Go figure.* But the camera did serve as a nice mirror when I needed one, which I did now. After inspecting my face, I surmised that I was not covered in ink. So what was everyone laughing about?

Mrs. Henley picked up her paperback copy of *The Great Gatsby* and held it up. Ignoring the funny feeling in the pit of my stomach and the light giggling in the background, I fished in my backpack for my copy of the book. When my fingers lighted on it, I yanked it out. It was tattered on the edges, its pages crinkled from years of use. This wasn't my first time reading the book. I was always several years ahead on our school reading lists. But I didn't mind. I liked re-reading books. I found that it gave me a better understanding, and I always learned new things in each reading. Novels were like that. There was so much to a story, so many nuances in the pages, so many hidden treasures, and a reader missed them if they only read the book one time.

"Nick Carraway, by his own admission, is an honest man. Do you think this is a correct assessment?" Mrs. Henley asked.

Glancing around, I waited for someone to raise their hand, but no one did. Mrs. Henley scoured the classroom, her gaze sweeping us. I slid lower in my chair when her eyes rested on me. It's not that I didn't have an answer, it's that I didn't want to draw attention to myself. Especially not today when everyone was already laughing at me.

"London, what do you think?"

Sitting up straighter, I took a deep breath and summoned up my courage. Lifting my chin, I said, "I don't think so. He stands by and watches all the deception around him and does nothing to stop it. In fact, in some instances he's an accomplice to the affairs and lies. I think standing idly by is just as bad as being the one doing the deceiving." My gaze shifted around the room at my fellow students. People I'd gone to school with for years. Not all of them had teased me, not all of them had bullied me. However, none of them had stuck up for me or helped me.

"Interesting assessment. Thank you, London," Mrs. Henley said. "There are many rumors surrounding Jay Gatsby. The fact that he neither confirms nor denies them, do you think this is a form of deception as well?"

Mrs. Henley called on a girl in the front row.

"Yes," the girl said.

"Really? Even though he's not the one spreading the rumors?" Mrs. Henley challenged her.

The girl shifted in her seat, as if re-thinking her answer. But I knew the girl's first answer was right. She shouldn't waffle. Gatsby was deceptive in allowing people to believe the rumors. In fact, I think he liked it. He liked being illusive, a mystery. In some ways I understood that about him. Sometimes the hardest person in the world to be is yourself.

After class, the giggling started back up again. This time it was in the hallway. People pointed and stared, chuckling. *What the hell?* Craning my neck, I tried to look at my back, but couldn't see anything. My cheeks hot, I lowered my head and hurried down the hall. I needed to get into a bathroom and find out what was wrong. As I walked swiftly, not looking at anyone, I remembered Calista touching my back. Pulse racing, I reached with my arm and felt the area where Calista had her hand. Sure enough, my fingers brushed over the edge of something sharp and thin. I tugged on it, and it came loose. *A post-it note.* Holding it between my fingers, I read the word scrawled in permanent marker.

SLUT

Very clever. Snorting, I crumpled it up and fisted it in my palm. Well, at least it was over now. I hoped everyone had a good laugh. Seething with anger, I stalked forward, my feet clicking on the slick floors. Snickering bounced around me like a beach ball being tossed at the beach. Reaching behind me, I grappled around my back looking for more post-its, but didn't feel any. Why were people still laughing?

"London." My head snapped up at Cooper's voice. "You okay?"

Confused, I stared up at his worried expression. What did he know?

He was at my house on Friday night. Calista's words sparked in my mind.

I stared at the yellow balled up paper in my hand. *Slut.* What an odd word to describe me. I was pretty sure in order to be a slut you'd have to do more than just read about sex. I'd never even kissed a boy, much less hooked up with one. So why would Calista think I was a slut?

When I glanced back up at Cooper I saw Gatsby. I saw deception and lies. And I didn't know what to think or who to believe anymore. I'd been bullied and picked on for years, but this felt different. It felt personal. And I knew that part of it was my fault. I'd allowed myself to feel something for Cooper that I shouldn't have.

"I have to go." It was lunch period and usually I sat with Skyler in the quad. Pushing past him, I went in search of her.

"London, wait." Cooper's hand clamped around my wrist.

I stiffened. "Let go."

"Please. I want to talk to you."

"About what?" I knew I should walk away, but curiosity kept me from moving.

"I don't know how she got the pictures, but I never told her anything was going on between us."

His words confused me. "Of course, because there *isn't* anything going on between us." I wriggled out of his grasp, and he released me. "Wait. What pictures?"

"You haven't seen them?"

"No." I shook my head, dread sinking into my gut.

"Don't you have Snap-It and Share-It?"

I shook my head. "All I know is that Calista stuck this to my back earlier." Unrolling my fingers, I exposed the crumpled post-it.

Cooper plucked it out of my palm and opened it up. Darkness flickered in his eyes, and his mouth pressed into a tight line. With his free hand, he shoved his fingers into the pocket of his jeans and extracted his cell phone. After typing in a few keys, he held it up for me to see.

My stomach plummeted as I took in the pictures posted on the Snap-It and Share-It site. One was of my back, the word slut taped to my shoulder. In the next one Cooper was walking me to class, holding my backpack, and in the other we were talking behind the bleachers. Only with the bleachers obscuring us, it appeared that we were doing more than talking. My stomach tightened. Below all the pictures the caption read: She acts like a good girl, but only Cooper knows how nasty she can be. Too bad she's still hung up on him since he's clearly moved on. Nerdgirl didn't realize she was just another notch in his belt.

The next picture was of Cooper and some girl kissing. She wore a tight shirt and tiny denim skirt. Her hands were up his shirt, and his fingers were tangled in her hair. I turned away, feeling sickened. Shoving the phone toward Cooper, I backed away from him.

"I'm really sorry," Cooper said, his eyes pleading with mine.

Without responding, I spun around and raced down the hallway. I knew it was a mistake to trust Cooper. From the minute he pulled over to help me, I suspected it was all some sort of game. The only reason I fell for his smooth lines and kind smile was because I desperately wanted to believe that he was a good guy, and that maybe, just maybe, he genuinely liked me. But I guess I'd been wrong.

I spent the rest of lunch period sitting alone on the floor in a back corner of the library, hidden behind a large bookshelf. The carpet was rough and smelled like feet. Still, it was better than being at the mercy of everyone out there. I'd never allowed them to see me crumble. I always stayed strong, but today I was worried I might lose it. And that was something I couldn't let happen. A few minutes before the bell rang, Skyler's head peeked around the corner.

"There you are." She let out a relieved sigh. "I've been looking everywhere."

"Well, now you found me."

"Why didn't you answer any of my texts?" She maneuvered around the bookshelf and plunked down on the ground beside me. Her long hair fell down her back in large curls. It smelled like hairspray and apple shampoo. "I was worried."

Guilt struck me. Skyler was a good friend, and I shouldn't have ignored her. I dropped my head onto her shoulder. "I'm sorry. I guess I needed some time alone."

"Did it help?"

"It helped me process things a little," I said. "The one thing I do know for sure is that I'll never trust another guy like Cooper again. No way will I ever be swayed by a guy just because he has dimples." The corner of my lip tugged upward.

I expected Skyler to laugh at this, but her face grew serious. "Didn't you read my texts?"

Shaking my head, I patted the front pocket of my backpack where my phone was safely nestled inside.

"London, you should've seen Cooper at lunch. He told Calista off and made her delete the pictures."

My body heated up. "He did?"

She nodded emphatically. "Yeah, he did." Then she slumped back, sighing. "God, it was so romantic."

Rolling my eyes, I groaned. "Everything is romantic to you."

"True." She sat up. "But this was honestly

the most romantic thing I've ever seen. Like as romantic as when Edward saves Bella from being hit by a car."

"Weird comparison, but okay." Skyler was obsessed with all things Twilight. I sometimes worried that she'd never be happy with any guy in real life because she compared them all to Edward. And let's face it, no real boy could compare to a fictional vampire. But I knew this wasn't at all like a scene from a romance novel. Cooper didn't defend me because he was into me. But then why did he? I thought back to our discussion in English class, how I'd been thinking about how no one ever stood up for me. But now Cooper had, and I didn't understand why.

CHAPTER 14
Cooper

"Dude, come on, you've got this!" Nate hollered from third base.

But he was wrong. I didn't have it. For some reason I couldn't get my shit together today. My mind was a jumbled mess. I couldn't focus. But I needed to soon or Coach was going to pull me. Closing my eyes, I drew in a deep breath, pulling it in through my nose and exhaling with my mouth. When I opened them, I locked eyes with the batter. *Okay, Cooper, you can do this.* I got into position and brought the ball into my chest. When I released it I knew instantly that it wasn't a good pitch. When the umpire called ball four, I groaned. I never walked guys. I struck them out. It's what I was good at. And it's what my team counted on.

After two more walks, the batter dropped the bat and jogged over to first base making it bases loaded. While the next batter headed out of the dugout, Nate jogged over to me.

"You all right, man?"

I nodded, blowing out a ragged breath. "I don't know what's wrong with me today."

"Well, you better figure it out."

"I will," I promised, even though I wasn't sure if I could keep it.

While he headed back to third, I faced the

batter.

I'm sure you'll get it together in time for Monday's game.

When I saw you play, you were incredible.

Shaking my head, I tried to get London's words out of my head, but they played over and over like a song on replay. I needed to stop thinking about her and get my head in the game. But she kept floating into my mind. And she was loud, damn it. I couldn't shut her off. It wasn't just her words, it was her face too. I pictured her large caramel colored eyes, her shimmery lips. I didn't know why she was taking over my thoughts like this. Remembering the angry expression she had after looking at those pictures Calista posted, my stomach clenched. If only she would've listened. If only I could've explained. I never meant for any of that to happen.

But it was clear she didn't want to hear anything I had to say. Not that I blamed her.

"C',mon, Coop." Nate's voice yanked me back to the game.

Never before had I had this much trouble concentrating. Frankly, it sucked. Attempting to quiet my racing thoughts, I honed in on the batter. He was a guy I'd struck out numerous times in the past, and I remembered his swing. Feeling confident, I threw the pitch. I felt better about this one than the others.

The batter swung, and the ball flew past me. Whirling around, I watched where it landed. Good thing Brandon was in the outfield and caught it. Luckily, it wasn't hit deep enough to score the runner from third. After he made a great throw to the cut-off man, I hopped up on the mound and my hope buoyed. But it quickly took a nosedive when the next batter hit a line drive over the second baseman's head for a single.

It didn't get any better as the inning progressed. By the time it was over, I'd allowed two more runs, and now we were losing the game. Shoulders slumping in defeat, I trudged toward the dugout. When I glanced up at the stands, only a few parents were sitting on the guest side. I was relieved that my grandparents weren't here to see this. Sometimes they came to our away games, but this one was a little too far for them. Besides, it was stinking hot out here. They were better off hanging out in the air-conditioned house. I sure as hell wouldn't be outside if I had a choice. Sweat slid out from under my hat and rolled down my face. Reaching up with my free hand, I wiped my skin. Not that it helped much. More sweat followed.

"It's okay." Nate sidled up next to me. "We'll get 'em next inning."

"I'm sure Coach'll pull me before that."

I was glad that Nate didn't bother to argue with me. We both knew what would happen. Thomas was already in the bullpen warming up his arm. *Damn it.*

"Wanna tell me what's going on?" Nate asked.

I shook my head. "Nothing. I just have a lot on my mind."

"This doesn't have anything to do with what happened today? With Calista and the newspaper chick?

Irritation bubbled inside of me like the carbonation in a soda. "Her name is London."

Nate threw up his arms as if he was involved in a stick up. "Hey, I don't know what's going on with you and London, but for the sake of your baseball career, you better work it out."

I nodded, knowing he was right. If I had any hope of getting my head on straight, I needed to face this.

After the game, I drove straight to her house. The sky was darkening, turning a deep blue, almost navy color. When I pulled up to the curb, my stomach knotted. I had a feeling she wasn't going to be happy to see me. However, I didn't have a choice. I had to talk to her, and it had to be now. Shutting off the engine, I threw off my seatbelt and stepped out of the car. It was cooling down, but it wasn't exactly cold yet. Still, goosebumps rose on my arm. My hair was damp from sweat under my hat, my shirt a little moist. Shoving the keys in my pocket, I slammed my car door shut and walked up the driveway. I'd changed out of my cleats and into a pair of tennis shoes, but I hadn't taken off my uniform yet.

After rapping on the door, it took only a few seconds for it to pop open. London's dad stood in the doorway, and I swallowed hard.

"Hi Mr.---" *Shit. What was London's last name?* "Miller," I practically shouted when I finally recalled it.

"Hi, Cooper." He nodded his head. "You

109

can call me Dexter."

Right. Dexter. He'd told me that. "Okay." I glanced over his shoulder, but the family room was empty. "Um…is London home?"

"Yeah. I'll get her." Dexter eyed me warily. "You want to come in?"

I hesitated, unsure if London would want me inside her house. She wasn't exactly my biggest fan right now. Remembering Emma's statement on Saturday caused a fresh wave of shame to descend on me. "Um…no, it's okay. I'll wait here."

"Suit yourself." He wore an amused expression as he turned around and walked away from me, leaving the front door open.

Nervous, I shook my leg while I waited. Less than a minute later, London appeared in front of me. She was wearing a pair of sweat pants and a t-shirt, her hair down, her face scrubbed clean. She smelled like soap.

"Hey," I greeted her.

"What are you doing here, Cooper?"

I wasn't expecting a warm welcome, but a little cordiality would have been nice.

"I need to talk to you," I said, and then wished I'd rehearsed something on the way over. Now that she was in front of me, I had no idea what I would say.

London peered over her shoulder and then sighed. "Okay. We can talk out here." Stepping outside, she closed the door behind her. Her toes were bare, her toenails painted pink. It seemed out of character for her, and it drew me to her in a weird way. Leaning against the house, she crossed her arms

110

over her chest. But not before I noticed she wasn't wearing a bra. Damn, first the bare feet and now this. I had to fight against the attraction I felt, and it confirmed what I already knew.

I wanted this girl. And I wanted her bad.

She cocked an eyebrow, waiting for me to speak.

I cleared my throat. "I played like shit today."

"Thanks for the report. I'll alert the media." Her statement was sarcastic, but her tone was detached; bored.

"It's your fault," I blurted out.

Her eyes widened. "Wow. Way to kick me when I'm down."

"Sorry," I mumbled. "I'm no good at words. That's your thing. What I'm trying to say is..." I stared at her, attempting to formulate my next statement.

London bit down on her lower lip, dragging it through her teeth.

Damn, it was all too much. There was only one way to get this chick out of my head. I stepped forward, curved my palm around her neck and drew her lips toward mine.

"Cooper." She threw her hands up, creating a wall between our faces. "What are you doing?"

Grunting, I moved away from her. "God, I'm totally screwing this up, aren't I?"

"Well, it's not going great."

I chuckled at her honest response. "You know, you're the first girl to ever turn down a kiss from me."

"Maybe give me some warning next time."

111

I froze. "Is that your way of telling me to try again?"

"Cooper." She sighed with exasperation. "You're not making any sense. What's going on?"

"I know, I know. I'm all over the place." I shook my head. "It's just that I've got all these thoughts swirling in my mind. I'm so confused. I-I." Pausing, I locked eyes with London. Taking a deep breath, I focused in on what I wanted to say the same way I focus during a game. I was pretty sure if I didn't dumb down the crazy a little bit, she'd head inside any minute. And I couldn't let that happen. I was on a mission, and I wasn't leaving until she heard me out. "I had nothing to do with those pictures. I need you to know that."

"I do."

"You do?"

She nodded. "Yeah. Skyler told me how you confronted Calista about them."

Relief washed over me, then it was replaced by confusion. "Then why are you still mad at me?"

"I'm not." She shrugged. "I'm not anything at you."

Her words pierced my heart, and I suddenly knew how every girl I'd brushed off felt. And it sucked. I didn't want to be nothing to London. When I stared into those amazing light eyes of hers, I knew why. It was because in her eyes I saw myself. I saw the sorrow that resided deep in my heart reflected back at me. London had been through the same kind of hell I'd been through, I was sure of it. And she'd survived. She'd clawed her way back to life. It was why she was so strong and determined.

112

I'd seen it when she'd sprained her ankle, and when she'd fallen at school, and when Calista posted the pictures online. The other girls I'd been with could hardly survive a hangnail. But London was tough.

"What can I do to be something to you?" I asked sincerely.

She narrowed her eyes. "Are you drunk?"

"No. I don't drink at my games. Although, today it might have helped," I joked.

"Is this a dare?"

Stepping forward, I caught her eyes. "Of course not. I would never do that."

"C'mon, Cooper. I'm not an idiot. I know what kind of reputation you have. Hell, I saw the picture of you all over some blond girl just this past weekend. And don't forget, I was an eye witness to the train wreck with Calista."

"I'm not gonna deny it. I've hooked up with a lot of girls. I never really thought it was a big deal until you called me on it last week. Now I feel pretty shitty about it." I searched her face, but it was unreadable. I hoped my words were hitting their mark; that I was getting to her. "The thing is that I've never wanted a relationship. I don't have time for one with baseball and school. Those are the things that are important to me."

"Then why hook up at all?"

"Because I'm a guy." I smiled, but she didn't return it.

"Well, I'm not like Calista or that girl from the picture. Contrary to popular belief, I'm not a slut. I'm sorry if Calista's little message on my back gave you the wrong impression."

113

"I know you're not."

"Then why did you try to kiss me?"

"I couldn't help myself." I reached for her, snatching up her hands. "You stir up these feelings inside of me that I don't understand. That's why I screwed up so bad at the game today, because I couldn't stop thinking about you."

She yanked back her arms, her hands slipping from mine. "I-I-have to go."

"London," I pleaded with her.

She shook her head as she reached for the doorknob.

I grabbed her around the waist, pressing my chest to her back. "Don't go yet."

"Get off me or I'll scream." The terror in her voice was real. Too real. *What the hell was wrong with me?* I was acting like a desperate lunatic tonight.

Shoving off of her, I felt like a dick. "I'm sorry. I didn't mean to frighten you."

Her response was the door slamming in my face after she'd raced inside. *That went well.*

CHAPTER 15
London

"London?" Dad entered the family room. "You okay?"

I stood with my back against the door, my heart pounding in my chest. Unable to speak, I nodded.

"What happened?"

I wasn't even sure. The whole exchange with Cooper had left me bewildered. His demeanor was nothing like the way he'd acted in our previous exchanges. I wasn't ruling out recreational drug use at this point.

"Speak, London." Dad stepped into the room, narrowing his eyes. Wrinkles formed around them. "You're scaring me."

It was then that I realized I was shaking. My hands quivered at my sides. "Nothing happened, Dad. I'm fine."

"You sure?"

I nodded. Outside I heard the sound of Cooper's car door opening and closing, followed by the car engine roaring to life.

"What did he want?" Dad nodded toward the window.

"I'm not sure."

Dad's lips curved upward in a teasing way. "He looked a little smitten to me."

My chest tightened. "He's not smitten. Also, no one uses the word 'smitten' anymore."

"Trust me. I know these things. I'm a guy too."

I shoved off the door still feeling a little unsteady on my feet. "Thanks for clarifying your gender with me."

He chuckled. "My daughter. Always the smart-alec."

I walked across the family room, suddenly very tired. "I think I've had enough excitement for one day. I'm gonna go to bed." After giving Dad a kiss on the cheek, my eyes grazed over Mom's picture. I shivered.

"What happened to your mom isn't going to happen to you, London."

His words startled me. "I know."

"Do you?" He eyed me knowingly. "Cooper seems like a nice boy. Don't push him away because of what happened in the past."

"I'm not," I said before shuffling briskly down the hallway. When I reached my room, I slipped inside and closed the door firmly. But even in the quiet of my room, Dad's words reached me, batting and clawing at me. Were they true? Was I pushing Cooper away because of Mom?

It was easy to assume it was my distrust of Cooper that kept me from giving in to him tonight. But my memory of Mom had always held me captive. Her grip on me was stronger now than it ever had been when she was alive. And that fateful day had lived in my mind like a living, breathing thing. It had shaped me into the person I was today. Much of my decisions and behaviors stemmed from that one moment in time. Above anything else that had ever happened to me, it was that day that defined me.

A song rang out in my quiet room, and I jumped, a squeal leaping from my throat. It took a minute to realize it was my phone. Racing to my dresser, I picked it up. Skyler's picture lit up on the screen.

"Hey, Skyler."

"What was Cooper doing at your house?"

"Who needs an alarm system with you around?" I teased. "You're a regular watchdog. If the neighbors ever come around wanting to start a neighborhood watch program, I'm sending them your way."

Skyler's giggle floated through the line. I leaned my back against the dresser, the knob of the drawer poking into my back.

"He looked hot in his baseball uniform," she said, and I didn't bother denying it. He *had* looked hot. "What did he want?"

"To tell me that he played shitty, and it was my fault."

"What?" She sounded as shocked as I felt when he first said it. "Okay, start at the beginning. I want to hear the whole thing."

Weariness was hitting me hard, and my eyelids were lowering. I wanted to stay up all night and chat with Skyler, but I was too damn tired. I'd been feeling this way a lot lately. Maybe I wasn't getting enough sleep. I vowed to go right to sleep tonight, and not pick up my Kindle at all.

"I'll tell you all about it tomorrow. I'm going

to bed."

"But it's only eight o'clock."

"Is it that early?" *Shit. It felt like midnight.* I yawned. "I haven't been sleeping well."

"Okay." She sighed heavily in the phone. "Fine, but I'll give you a ride. I'm not waiting until lunch to hear about this."

"Deal." Usually I protested when Skyler offered to give me a ride, but the truth was that the bike rides were getting more tedious with each passing day. This morning I even had to stop to catch my breath after riding up a hill. Man, I sounded like an old woman. I needed some serious sleep tonight so I could get my energy back.

After hanging up with Skyler, I sank down onto my bed and stared out the window. The sky was dark, the crescent moon illuminating it with bright yellow light. My skin buzzed where Cooper had touched me. Reaching up, I ran my fingers along my lips, wondering what it would have felt like to have Cooper's lips on mine. Would it have been so bad to let him kiss me? I'd never been kissed before, so I didn't even know what I was missing.

There are worse guys to have your first kiss with than Cooper Montgomery.

From that first day I'd hiked out to the baseball field to interview Cooper I'd been attracted to him. Even though I'd tried to deny it, it was true. But he confused the hell out of me. I could never figure him out.

You stir up these feelings inside of me that I don't understand.

Well, that made two of us.

118

The insistent buzzing woke me. My eyelids fluttered open, and I reached out expecting to touch my alarm clock. But my fingers skimmed my bedspread. My body ached, my neck kinked. When I opened my eyes all the way, they felt sticky and dry. The alarm clock still blared, so I rolled over trying to locate it. Crawling forward on my bed, I swung my arm out. My palm connected with the button, and the noise ceased. Glorious silence blanketed me. The room came into focus, and I blinked, confused. Oh shit. Had I forgotten to take out my contacts?

Glancing down, I realized I was wearing the same clothes I had on last night. I must have fallen asleep right after my conversation with Skyler. Sure enough, my phone was exactly where I'd left it on my dresser. The battery was probably dead by now. Wow, I really must have been tired. At least I got a good night's sleep. Now maybe I wouldn't be so exhausted today. Although even as I thought it, I knew that I didn't feel as rested as I should. Pushing myself up, my joints cracked. Yawning, I tossed my legs off the bed. My feet hit the carpet, the soft reeds brushing my heels. Standing, I moved toward my dresser. When my gaze found my reflection, I cringed. Lines from the bedspread ran over my flesh, and my hair was stuck to my head like it had been glued that way. A shower was unavoidable this morning. Heading across the hallway toward the bathroom, memories of last night crashed over me. A small smile drifted over my lips, and I knew I was in big trouble.

Standing under the spray of the shower, I wondered if Cooper would even speak to me today after I'd pushed him away last night. A part of me hoped he'd ignore me. It would make all of this easier. I knew that I wouldn't have enough willpower to turn him down a second time. No matter the consequences, if he came on to me again, I knew I'd take him up on his offer.

By the time I finished getting ready, Dad was leaving for work. When I entered the kitchen to make my lunch, he glanced over at me with one eyebrow raised.

"You look nice."

"You sound surprised."

"Not surprised, pumpkin. You always look beautiful."

My cheeks warmed at his words. Reaching into the cabinet, I dragged out the loaf of bread.

"You just don't normally dress like that."

After setting down the loaf of bread, I glanced down at the red top, skinny jeans, and silver sandals I had on. The sandals I had worn for my cousin's wedding last summer, and the red top was one Skyler insisted I buy on our last trip to the mall. I had to cut the tag off of it this morning.

Opening the fridge, I shrugged. "Just felt like wearing something a little different. Besides, Skyler's giving me a ride, so I don't have to wear my tennis shoes."

"This wouldn't have anything to do with a certain baseball player, would it?"

Now my cheeks felt like they were on fire. With trembling hands, I pulled out the lunch meat and mayonnaise. "No, it wouldn't."

"Okay. If you say so." Dad grabbed his lunch off the counter. "Have a good day, pumpkin."

My hands full, I closed the fridge door with my hip. Then I dropped the contents on the counter. "You too."

After Dad left, I hurriedly finished making my lunch. Then I headed outside to meet Skyler. When I stepped onto my front porch, my breath hitched in my throat. Standing in my driveway leaning against his parked car, was Cooper. He wore a pair of jeans and a grey t-shirt that perfectly molded to his taut chest. Covering his blond hair was a navy blue baseball hat. It made his blue eyes stand out even more than usual.

"What are you doing here?"

"Is that how you're always going to greet me?" He shoved off the car, and stepped forward.

"Sorry. I wasn't expecting you." My gaze flitted next door. "Skyler was giving me a ride."

"Not anymore. She said it was cool if you rode with me."

"She did?" I caught sight of Skyler peeking out the window. She gave me a smile and a thumbs up sign. I almost laughed out loud.

"Yeah. She came out a few minutes ago." His gaze roved over my body. "You look hot."

I inhaled sharply. "Hot?" No one had ever said that to me before.

"Yeah. Normally you look pretty. Today you look hot."

"Y-y-you normally think I look pretty?" My head was spinning, and for a minute I wondered if I was still asleep in my bed dreaming. None of this felt real.

"Absolutely." He nodded. "Why does that surprise you?"

"I guess because no one has ever said it before." I paused, remembering my conversation with my dad. "Well, except my dad."

"We've got to change that." He smiled.

I swallowed back the emotion that rose in my throat.

"I'm sorry about last night," he said.

"You are?" I frowned, wondering if I misread everything.

He took another step until he was so close I could smell the toothpaste on his breath, the faint scent of deodorant, and soap on his skin. "Not sorry about what I said. I meant every word. But I'm sorry I came on so strong." Slowly he lifted his arm, keeping his gaze trained on me as if gauging my reaction. I stayed calm, standing still like a statue. When his fingers swept across my chin, I didn't flinch. "I didn't mean to scare you, London. I never want to scare you."

The fear that inhabited my heart fought its way out, but I shoved it back down. Not today. Not now. I would listen to my dad, and listen to my heart. I wouldn't allow what happened to Mom ruin this for me.

"I'm sorry too. I shouldn't have pushed you away." I started to lower my gaze, but his fingers gently forced my head back up.

"Are you saying that if I try to kiss you again you won't stop me this time?"

My heart clattered in my chest, and my palms moistened. *Was that I was saying?* Dear god, I didn't know.

Panic must have registered on my face because Cooper cocked his head to the side. "London, you've never been kissed before, have you?"

I shook my head.

"Ah, now I really feel like a dick." He withdrew his hand from my face.

"Why?" Already, I missed his touch.

"Because your first kiss should be amazing." He smiled. "And I'm going to make sure it is."

"What makes you so sure it's going to be with you?" I teased.

"Oh, trust me. It'll be with me."

At his confidence I couldn't help but feel a little giddy. And when I got into his car, my mind spun with the possibilities. As much as I wanted him to kiss me now, I knew waiting was best. I had only come to terms with my feelings for him last night. I needed to give it time. I needed to be sure. Not only that, but I needed to know that he was sure. As we pulled into the school parking lot, I knew this would be the true test. It was one thing for Cooper to think he had feelings for me when it was the two of us. Would he feel the same way at school in front of our peers and his friends? Would he feel that way when he compared me to the popular girls he normally dated?

I wasn't so sure, and my stomach rolled with doubt and worry. Reaching down, I picked up my backpack and hoisted it into my lap.

"Hey." His hand rested on my thigh.

My pulse spiked.

"Tell me why you don't use your locker," he said, his question surprising me.

"Um…I just don't like to."

"Why don't you like to?"

I shifted in the seat, noticing the time on his dashboard. "Crap. I have to get to class."

His grip on my thigh tightened. "Please tell me why."

"My locker is right next to Calista's, and she sort of bothers me every time I try to use it. Sometimes she and her friends stand in front of my locker refusing to move, and I end up being late for class. Or she makes rude remarks about my clothes." Feeling like an idiot, I bit my lip. I wouldn't be stunned if he changed his mind about me at this point. I sounded like a whiny kid. "It's no big deal. I find it's easier to avoid the entire thing by carrying my books around."

His jaw tensed, his facial expression hardening. "And this is the girl you were defending to me?"

And this is the girl you were hooking up with last week? Was what I wanted to say, but I held the words inside. But, as I thought them, I wondered if this was a mistake. I was so quick to jump in with both feet when he showed up at my house this morning. Normally I was so cautious, and maybe I needed to be that way now. By his own admission, he used girls. Was I just another girl to be used? I wasn't sure I could handle that.

"What class do you have for zero period?"

124

His question broke into my internal thoughts.

"Mr. Grant."

"Okay. I'll meet you at Mr. Grant's classroom before first period. Wait for me." He squeezed my thigh. "I'll walk you to your locker."

My heart skipped a beat, my earlier misgivings falling away. It was like Cooper was my own personal savior.

CHAPTER 16
Cooper

London was standing outside of Mr. Grant's classroom, her gaze shifting around nervously as I approached. When her eyes met mine, the relief inside them was evident. It cut to my heart. Did she think I wouldn't show? That I would flake on her? Was her opinion of me that low? A few students whisked past, one girl throwing a disgusted look London's way. I caught the slight frown on London's face, the tremor of her hands, and realization slammed into me. Her doubt had nothing to do with her opinion of me. It had to do with her opinion of herself. And that hurt me even more. In the short time that I'd known London, I'd grown to respect and admire her. It sickened me that she didn't know how amazing she was. And it sickened me further to know that up until now I had contributed to her feeling this way.

But no more. Things would change today.

"Hey," I stood next to her, offering her my arm. "Ready?"

A look of awe passed over her features that made me want to grab her and kiss her right here. It took all my willpower not to. But I had promised her an amazing first kiss, and that wouldn't be in the middle of a stinky high school hallway. With other girls I always felt they were drawn to my popularity,

126

my looks, or my social status. With London I could tell she was drawn to me - just me. I think I saw it that first day at the baseball field, the way she looked at me with real interest. And that was something I wanted more of.

She smiled, looping her arm in mine. "Sure."

Her hand felt good resting in the crook of my arm, her fingers fluttering over my skin. It caused desire to rise inside of me, and it was difficult to temper. Man, who knew London Miller could ever elicit these kinds of feelings in me. If someone had told me weeks ago that I would feel this way about her, I would've laughed my ass off. But now I wasn't laughing. Not one bit.

We rounded the corner, and London pointed out her locker to me. Calista was standing in front of it chatting with Chloe, Brooke, and Lauren. My stomach twisted when Calista's gaze landed on London and me. Her mouth gaped open, her eyes narrowing. Reaching out, she latched onto Lauren's arm and whispered something. Pretty soon all four girls were staring at us. London's face remained unreadable, her gaze fixed ahead. Pride swelled inside of me.

Brooke was leaning against London's locker when we reached it. London glanced up at me as if she was unsure of what to do. It irritated me that they had made her feel like she couldn't use her own goddamn locker. And to think these were the people I'd hung out with for the past four years. What made us think we owned the whole freaking school?

"Excuse me," I said to Brooke, shooing her away with my hand. "Go lean against your own locker. This is London's."

Brooke pursed her lips and glared at me, hard. But she moved. Slowly, but still. As London punched in her code with a shaky hand, I leaned against the locker next to hers, my body shielding her from Calista and her friends. After the door rattled open, London extracted several books from her backpack and set them inside.

"What's he doing with *her*?" Brooke's voice sounded from over my shoulder. It was clear they were talking about London, and it was painfully obvious that they were talking loud enough for her to hear on purpose. God, could they be more transparent? Had I really thought those girls were sexy at some point? What had I been thinking?

London winced, but continued arranging the books in her locker.

"It was inevitable. He's already gone through all of us. It makes sense that he's moved on to the losers now," Calista said.

London bristled, her eyes bouncing to mine. I read the question in them and wished I could deny what Calista had said. But I couldn't. As embarrassed as I was to admit it, I had fooled around with all four of the girls who'd been tormenting London at her locker. But I wouldn't let them use it against London. And I wouldn't let them put a wedge between us already.

"Ignore them," I said to London.

She nodded, slamming her locker shut. After throwing her backpack over her shoulder, a small smile played on her lips. "Wow, it's so light."

"That's how it should be." I offered her my

128

arm again. "Where to?"

"You don't have to walk me to class. I can get there on my own," she said.

"I know, but I want to."

She bit her lip, and I anxiously awaited her response, wondering if she was already changing her mind about giving me a chance. I wouldn't blame her if she was.

Finally she said, "Okay." Then she snaked her arm through mine. "My next class is Mr. Carter's."

I had him last year, and hated his class. "Man, it's like they gave you all the hard-ass teachers."

She shrugged. "I can handle it."

"I bet you can." I smiled.

As we walked forward, I ignored the curious looks from the other students. Coming up on Mr. Carter's classroom, I passed Nate.

"Hey, Coop." He fist bumped me. "What's up?" His gaze slid past me to London, and then his brows raised. My chest tightened, waiting for the look of shock or disgust. But he did neither. Instead he nodded, flashing me a grin. "All right. Looks like you got your head on straight, man."

And that was why Nate was my best friend. He knew me like no other. "Yeah, I think I do."

"Cool. I'll see ya later." He nodded toward London. "You too, newspaper chick."

London raised her eyebrows.

"He likes giving people nicknames," I explained, my insides coiling. *Why did he call her that to her face?* It's not like she knew what he was like, and she hadn't exactly had the warmest welcome from our group. I was sure she was thinking the worst right now.

"Well, not everyone," he explained. "Just the cool people." With a wink, he walked off. Gratitude swept over me. London stared at him wearing a stunned expression. I smiled, looking from her to Nate, feeling like I'd finally made wise choices when it came to those I'd allowed into my life. I'd spent so many years keeping people at a distance, but I didn't want to do that anymore. I was ready to take a risk, even if it meant putting my heart on the line.

When I stepped into the house after practice, Grandma was in the dining room setting plates on the table. Our house had a great room floor plan, so the dining room was visible from the front door. I dropped my bag on the ground and walked across the room, stamping footprints over the newly vacuumed carpet. It smelled like roasted chicken, and faintly like vanilla. Following the sweet scent, a candle burned in the center of the dining table.

"You look happy," Grandma observed. "Practice must have went well."

"It did." I kissed Grandma on the cheek.

She set the last plate down with a soft thud. "I'm glad to hear it."

"I thought I heard you come in." Grandpa stepped into the room. "How was practice today?"

Grandma retreated back into the kitchen, and the sound of dishes clanging reached my ears.

"Great." I smiled, relieved to finally give him a good report. It had been brutal to tell him about the last couple of practices and games. "All my pitches were moving, and it felt like I was throwing it pretty hard."

"That's my boy." Grandpa slapped me good-naturedly on the back. "What changed, do you think?"

I knew exactly what changed. By finally facing my feelings for London, I could concentrate. But I didn't know how to say the words. Girls were not something I usually talked about with Grandpa.

I shrugged, an involuntary smile sweeping across my face. "Just got my head on straight, I guess."

"Did someone help you get it on straight?" Grandpa gave me a knowing look.

I scratched the back of my neck, sweat gathering under my nails. "Um…yeah, kind of."

"This someone wouldn't happen to be a girl, would it?"

Was it really that obvious? My lips tugged at the corners. "Maybe."

"I thought so." Grandpa glanced toward the kitchen. "You were behaving the same way I did when I met your grandma."

As if on cue, Grandma entered the room carrying a large platter of chicken. She always cooked enough for a dinner party even though it was only the three of us. My dad had been one of four siblings, so Grandma was used to cooking for a large family. It was like she had no idea how to make less. I didn't mind though. After a game or practice I could usually pack it away. And what I didn't eat, I could snack on late at night or have for lunch the next day. Take it from me, no food was wasted around here.

"You never told me about this." I leaned forward curiously

"Oh, yeah," Grandma interjected, placing the platter in the center of the table. "It's a good thing your grandpa finally asked me out. If he hadn't, he might have been benched for the remainder of the season."

"Really?" I asked.

Grandpa nodded. "Once this woman got into my mind, I couldn't get her out." He held out his arm and Grandma walked right into it. Even after all these years they were so in love. My parents were like that too. It was one of the reasons I'd never searched it out. I knew what it was like to suffer loss, to have someone cruelly ripped from your life. To have your heart broken in such a way that it will never be put back together again.

And I didn't know if I'd survive a second time.

But now as I watched Grandpa kiss Grandma's head, watch him pull her close, watch her smile in response, I found myself wanting that. Wanting someone who loved me unconditionally. Wanting to kiss someone, to hold someone, to make love to someone and know that it wasn't a one-time thing. To know that it meant something, that it mattered.

CHAPTER 17
London

Warm wind feathered over my skin as I pedaled quickly around the corner. My tires spun with ease along the trail. Trees lined both sides of the path, their branches leaning down over me as if they were arms reaching out. I was grateful for the shade since the sun was already warm this morning. Cooper rode next to me, our tires in sync.

I was pleased when he invited me on a bike ride today. Usually I spent my Saturdays curled up on the couch with a novel. For the first time in my life I had something else I'd rather do. I suppose I was realizing that living a romance was more exciting than reading about one. And no one was more surprised by this than me. Okay, well, maybe Dad.

He was literally in shock when I told him my plans for the weekend. I mean, he knew about Cooper. Ever since the night Cooper randomly showed up at our house, I'd been open with Dad about the situation. But things were progressing pretty rapidly. Our relationship felt a lot like a bike ride, like when you reached a steep hill and glided down so fast you knew you should hit the brakes, but you didn't want to because you enjoyed the rush of it. That's how it was with Cooper and me. It was like we both got on that hill and neither of us wanted to press on the brakes or pull over to the side.

He'd been driving me to school every day. Usually I had to ride home with Skyler, though, since Cooper had baseball. And he'd been walking me to my locker and classes. Lunchtime was the only awkward part. It was clear that I'd never fit in with his group. Nate was cool, but the rest of them stared at me as if I was one of those pictures where you pick out the thing that doesn't belong. And Calista's hatred of me seemed to be growing every day. A part of me felt nervous about how that would escalate. Cooper wasn't going to be able to be with me all the time. He couldn't protect me every second of everyday. And I'd witnessed how mean Calista could be. Therefore, I wasn't putting anything past her.

When the trail wound to the right, the lake came into view. It shimmered in the sunlight, its surface like glass. Ducks glided along the surface, their white feathers turning brown at the edges from the water. Kayakers rowed past us in their brightly colored boats. Algae hugged the rocks that dotted the shore, water splashing against the sides.

No matter how many times I saw the lake, it always took my breath away. "So beautiful," I breathed.

"Why don't we stop here," Cooper suggested. "Get a drink of water."

We hadn't been riding very long, and the trail we were on was easy, mostly flat surfaces. Still, I was getting winded. Much more so than usual. I told myself it was Cooper's proximity that was causing it.

Nodding, I guided my bike toward the sand off to the right side of the trail. After stopping, I hopped off my bike and set it on its kickstand. Then

I yanked off my helmet and set it down. Cooper did the same and then handed me my water bottle. I wrapped my hand around it noticing that my breathing was much more labored than Cooper's. In fact, he didn't appear to be fazed at all. It was probably from all that baseball playing. It made sense that he'd be in better shape than me. That's what I got for dating a baseball player.

"You all right?" He eyed me.

God, did I really seem that out of shape? I made a mental note to work out more often.

"Yeah, I'm fine."

"Okay." He didn't appear entirely convinced. "You just look a little pale."

"I do?" Reaching up, I touched my face. It was warm to the touch, and I did feel a little dizzy. Man, I really hoped I wasn't getting sick. I sort of felt like I'd been fighting off an illness for awhile. Maybe I'd feel better if I drank something. After bringing the water bottle to my lips, I took a sip, savoring the cool liquid as it swam down my throat. I hadn't realized how thirsty I was until now. Cooper took a swig from his water bottle too.

"Better?" He asked when I lowered the bottle from my lips.

"Yeah. I probably needed to hydrate." I brought the water bottle to my mouth again, but this time I sucked in too large of a gulp and water dribbled down my chin.

Before I could wipe it away, Cooper reached out and brushed the liquid off with his finger. I inhaled sharply. His gaze collided with mine, his hand curving around my face, his fingers slipping

135

into my hair. They massaged into my scalp, causing chills to skitter down my back. His face grew serious, his eyes darkening. In a lot of the romance novels I'd read, the author used the word 'smolder,' but I'd never understood that term. What did it mean when someone's eyes smoldered? Did their irises resemble a fire, complete with red flames? I wasn't sure. But now I knew what it looked like. And no, it wasn't like flames. It was like desire, it was like need. He brought his other hand up to frame my face, but his eyes never left mine. I was frozen in place, a giant block of ice on the side of the bike trail. In the distance I could hear bike tires rolling along, the quacking of ducks, the splashing of water. But none of it registered. Not with Cooper's hands on my face, with his eyes on mine. I knew where this was headed, and I didn't want to mess it up. I wanted it to happen. Cooper had been waiting to make it amazing, but I had no doubt that any kiss would be amazing with Cooper. His face angled slightly, tilting. His top lip brushed mine. Softly. Slowly. It was so gentle I could almost mistake it for the breeze. My arms were still pinned at my sides, my right one gripping tightly to the water bottle. The condensation coated my palm, dripping from my fingers. I longed to reach out and touch Cooper, to hold him, to run my hands along his waist, but I didn't have the courage to do it. I was so afraid to do something wrong that I stood completely still, waiting for him to guide me. He knew what he was doing. He'd kissed many girls.

At that thought my stomach soured, and I almost pulled away. I wondered what I was doing here with a guy who used girls, who I had been

136

calling a womanizer for years. But then his lips pressed down more firmly, and my head swirled. I didn't care who else he'd kissed, who else he'd been with. With his mouth touching my lips and his hands tangled in my hair, I didn't care about anything else. Nothing mattered except for this moment. For once in my life I wanted to throw caution to the wind, to embrace the present, not worrying at all about the past or the future. To not weigh every pro and con, but to simply live in the now.

His lips were soft and moist as they moved deftly over mine. It was clear he was no novice. When his tongue skimmed my lips, I took his cue, carefully parting them. His tongue thrust inside, sliding over my tongue. I could no longer keep my arms down. I had to touch him. Dropping the water bottle into the sand, I lifted my arms to his waist. I slid them around his middle, clutching him tightly. His hands tunneled my hair, cupping the back of my head firmly as the kiss deepened in intensity. The kiss was languid as Cooper took his time, making every caress, every movement matter. There were moments in the past week where I'd questioned Cooper's feelings for me. Doubts crept in, making me wonder if I was being naïve to start falling for him. But in this moment those doubts flew away. In his kiss I felt his passion, and I knew it was real.

When he drew back, I sucked in a breath, feeling dizzy. Cooper's hands slid out of my hair and down my back. He glanced around guiltily.

"Sorry. The side of the bike trail probably wasn't the most romantic place for our first kiss." His gaze lowered to my lips. "I couldn't hold back anymore."

"It was perfect," I said.

He smiled. "It was perfect, wasn't it?"

I giggled, glad I didn't mess it up too bad.

"You know, I sort of feel like I've been lied to," Cooper said, causing the smile to vanish from my face. *What was he talking about?* "There's no way that was your first kiss."

"It was. I swear."

"Well, then you're a natural."

"I wasn't terrible at it?"

"Terrible?" One side of his mouth curled upward. "Nope. Not at all. Try mind-blowing."

"Mind-blowing?" I shook my head. "Now you're being crazy."

He tugged me forward. "Are you saying that it wasn't mind-blowing for you? Because if not, I'll take that as a challenge. I'll show you mind-blowing."

"Oh, you will, huh?"

His lips neared mine, and my heart picked up speed. "Yeah, I will." A puff of hot air met my lips. His mouth claimed mine with even more intensity than the last time, while his hands raked up my back, his fingers trailing over my spine. I fisted the bottom of his shirt in between my fingers in an attempt to steady myself as his tongue forced open my lips and darted into my mouth. This kiss was rapid and more desperate. It felt like he was breathing life into me, but at the same time taking the oxygen he needed. This time when he pulled away his forehead dropped to mine. Both of our chests heaved, our breath coming out ragged. "How about now?" He said between gulps of air. "Mind-blowing?"

"Definitely," I said, causing him to smile.

A few minutes later we hopped back on our bikes and resumed our ride. Cooper had promised me lunch afterward, but I wasn't that hungry. The truth was that I hadn't been that hungry lately. I think I'd been too excited about Cooper to eat. Still, I'd join him for lunch. Anything to spend more time with him.

We rounded a corner leaving the lake behind us and entering a tunnel of trees. They swayed overhead as if they were dancing to a song only they could hear. Sweat gathered on my forehead, and my heart hammered as I struggled to keep riding. Already I was winded again. God, I hadn't realized how out of shape I was until today. I forced myself to keep riding, too embarrassed to tell Cooper. I'd bragged about my stellar bike riding abilities before we'd left for our ride today. I didn't want to admit that I was actually so out of shape that an easy, flat bike trail was too much for me.

Dread sank into my gut when I noticed we were approaching a hill. Fighting against the weariness, I pumped my legs harder, steeling myself for the incline. Cooper was ahead of me, and he rode up the hill with ease. I pedaled as hard as I could, but found myself struggling. My lungs felt like they were on fire, and breathing was so difficult it concerned me. When I got halfway up the hill, I couldn't go any farther. *What the hell was wrong with me?* After slamming on the brakes, I guided my bike into the sand at the right of the trail, attempting to catch my breath. Leaning over, I clutched my knees and breathed deeply, in and out.

"London?" Cooper raced over to me. After getting off his bike, he dropped it on the ground, and it landed with a loud clatter. Then he touched my back. "You okay?"

"I must be coming down with something. I've been feeling off all week." Peering up at him, I smiled wanly. "Probably should've told you that before you kissed me, huh?"

"There are worse ways to get sick." He shrugged. "Besides, it was worth it."

I smiled, but inside I was irritated. What a crappy time to get sick.

"Can you make it to my car? We're almost there. We parked around this corner."

Feeling like an idiot, I nodded. "I'll walk my bike up the hill and then ride it the rest of the way."

"Okay. I'll stay right beside you." He grabbed his bike off the ground, and together we walked our bikes up the hill. "Is your dad home?"

I shook my head. "I think he's at his friend's house watching the game."

"Then I'll come over and take care of you until your dad gets home."

"You don't have to do that." We reached the top of the hill, and I climbed back on my bike.

"I want to." He nudged me in the side before hopping up onto his bike seat. "Besides, you did promise to spend the day with me."

"That's right. I did, didn't I?" I pedaled slowly forward.

Cooper stayed right next to me. Other bikers zipped past, their wheels whispering as they rode. A gentle breeze floated over my body. We didn't have to ride very far before the trail ended. We turned the corner and rode across the parking lot to Cooper's car.

After loading our bikes on top, Cooper drove us back to my house. Dad was gone like I'd suspected, so Cooper stayed with me. He made me lie down on the couch, but the truth was that I was feeling a little better. Just kind of tired, but nothing like I'd felt on the trail. Sitting next to my legs, he reached over and placed his hand on my forehead.

"What are you doing?"

"Checking your temperature." He lifted his hand. "You don't feel warm. I mean, maybe a little sweaty from the ride, but not feverish."

"I'm impressed, Dr. Montgomery." I teased.

He chuckled. "What can I say? My grandma takes good care of me when I'm sick, so I learned from the best."

Cooper mentioned his grandparents a lot, but he never talked about his parents. I bit my lip, knowing I had to tread carefully with my next statement. "Your grandma, huh? Do your grandparents live with you or something?"

"Actually, I live with them." His gaze lowered, his hand finding mine. He ran his fingers over my flesh. "I have ever since my parents died."

I gasped. "I had no idea."

"It's not something I like to talk about."

"I'm sorry," I mumbled. "Then let's talk about something else. The bike ride was fun. Well, until I couldn't get up that hill. That was crazy, right?"

He squeezed my hand. "London, it's all right.

141

I don't mind talking to you about it. I want you to know about me."

"Are you sure?" I bit my lip.

He grinned. "You bite your lip when you're nervous."

"Is that a bad thing?"

"Nope. A good thing. A really good thing." He stared into my eyes as if trying to read something inside of them. "I never noticed things like that about a girl before, but with you I notice things. I love learning new things about you. I want to know everything about you, London, and I want you to know about me." His fingers threaded through mine. "Usually when a girl tries to pry into my personal life I shut down. I'm not going to do that with you." Lifting our hands, he ran his lips across my knuckles. "I'll always be open with you about everything. I promise."

"I bet you say that to all the girls." I was only half teasing. This whole thing was surreal to me. In all my years of high school, no boy had been attracted to me. Now suddenly Cooper Montgomery was kissing me and making me promises. It seemed too good to be true.

"Trust me, I don't. I've never said these things to any other girl."

"Why me?"

"You're different from any girl I've ever met."

I snorted, having heard that before.

"Hey, I meant that in a good way," he clarified. "You make me feel things. Things I've never felt before."

142

"You too." If he was going to bear his soul to me, I might as well do the same.

He reached out with his free hand and brushed a stray hair from my face. "When I was ten my parents left for a trip to Hawaii for their anniversary. I was going to stay with my grandparents for the week that they were gone. But there was a problem with the plane, some malfunction with one of the wings."

My stomach tightened as he spoke. I stroked his palm with my thumb, a silent encouragement.

"The plane crashed, and they didn't survive." Sadness flickered in his eyes. "I've lived with my grandparents ever since."

"I'm so sorry," I spoke softly. "I know how hard it is to lose someone you love."

"I know. It's one of the reasons I feel so connected to you."

CHAPTER 18
Cooper

I didn't regret telling her about my parents. In fact, I felt lighter since I'd shared it with her. Even though I normally avoided the subject at all costs, I meant what I said to London. I wanted her to know me. It was the first time in my life I desired to open up to anyone, let alone a girl. And I loved that she didn't offer me platitudes. Instead, she responded with empathy and sincere sorrow for my loss. It confirmed my decision to share with her. She understood me like I knew she would.

"Are you feeling any better?" I asked her.

"A little."

"Hungry?"

She shook her head.

I was freaking starving. How could she not be hungry? If I didn't like her so damn much I would hightail it out of here right now and head straight for the nearest fast food place. As if in reply to my thoughts, my stomach growled.

London giggled, staring at my tummy. "I can make you something to eat."

"I'm supposed to be taking care of you, not the other way around."

"It's no big deal." London sat up.

I gently pushed her back down. "No way. You're supposed to be resting."

She rolled her eyes, but a hint of a smile played on her lips. "Well, if you won't let me make you something, then go ahead and get something yourself. I won't have you starving to death on my couch."

"Is it my death that worries you or the idea of it happening on your couch?" I teased.

"Both," she joked back, but I caught a glimpse of something disturbing in her eyes. A glimmer of pain and regret.

"Okay. Point me in the right direction."

"Depends on what you feel like. There's sandwich stuff in the fridge, and chips and fruit on the counter."

"All right. That'll work." I headed into the kitchen and grabbed a handful of chips. It wouldn't fill me up, but at least it would tide me over for a bit. Chips in hand, I returned to London, plunking down onto the couch next to her legs. It wasn't the most comfortable place to sit since half my ass was hanging off the side, but I liked being close to her. It was like when I was a little boy and I used to sit next to my mom. I'd snuggled up so close I'd practically be in her lap. She used to tease me by pointing to the remainder of the couch, stating that there was tons of room. But what she didn't realize was that I was precisely where I wanted to be. I took a bite of one of the greasy potato chips, and it snapped in between my teeth. "You sure you don't want anything?" The gentleman in me hated eating in front of her like this. My grandma would never put up with this kind of behavior.

"I'm fine. I actually feel better knowing that

you won't be starving to death anytime soon."

"I give you my solemn promise that I won't. And if I do, I promise to move away from the couch."

She giggled, but a yawn escaped on the tail end of it. "God, I don't know why I'm so tired."

"There is a bug going around school," I reminded her.

Smiling, she said, "Yeah, I know all about it. You know that the only reason I interviewed you for the paper was because Annabelle Garcia had the flu."

"Really?" I raised an eyebrow, unsure of how Annabelle having the flu would cause London to interview me. Also, who the hell was Annabelle?

"She was supposed to do your article, but since she was gone John made me do it."

"*Made* you do it, huh?" I threw another chip into my mouth.

"If Annabelle hadn't been sick, you might be sitting in her living room right now."

"I highly doubt that."

She shrugged. "You never know."

But she was wrong. I did know. Whoever Annabelle was, she wouldn't have had this effect on me. I was sure of that. As I popped another chip into my mouth, my gaze rested on the picture hanging above the couch. It stirred a sense of déjà vu, and I realized that Grandma had hung a similar one in the guest bathroom. She bought it because she said it reminded her of her trip to London.

London. Huh.

"So what's the deal with your name?" I asked.

"You don't like it?"

"I love it. I just wondered what the significance of it was."

Pink spots rose on her cheeks. "Um...my parents took a trip there exactly nine months before I was born."

"Ah." I nudged her. "Looks like you and I are taking a trip to London."

She giggled, then sobered up, flinching out of nowhere. Glancing down, she reached into her pocket. "Text," she explained, yanking out her cell phone. She looked at the screen and then typed something with her thumbs. "That was Dad. He's on his way back. So, you only have to babysit me for a few more minutes and then you're off the hook." Smiling, she shoved the phone back into her pocket.

"Are you kidding? This is the best gig I've had in a long time. I wish I didn't have pitching lessons tomorrow so I could come back here and do more of this." I leaned forward, pressing my lips to hers. Her arms came around my neck, drawing me forward. My hands fumbled in her hair and slid down to her neck as my tongue teased her lips open. If I thought our first two kisses were mind-blowing, this one was even better. Before London was a little tentative, allowing me to lead. But this time she was bolder, sliding her tongue over mine and kissing me with fervor. Her hands skimmed over my neck, her fingers raking over my hair. When we separated, I blew out a breath. "Is that kiss your way of persuading me to cancel my lesson tomorrow?"

She giggled, leaning her head back down against the cushions. "Nah. It doesn't matter anyway.

I'm going to be swamped with homework. I have a science project due on Monday, and I haven't even started it."

Surprised, I cocked an eyebrow. "I never would've pegged you as a procrastinator."

"I'm not, but someone has kept me preoccupied this week."

I finished off the last chip, and rubbed my palms together in an effort to wipe away the grease. "I wouldn't be too hard on that someone. You are pretty damn irresistible."

"Irresistible. Yeah, right." She snorted, running a hand over her head. "Trust me, plenty of guys have resisted me."

"Hey." I placed my hand over hers. "Don't do that. I don't give out compliments lightly, so if I give you one, I mean it."

Her face grew serious, and she nodded.

"I have something for you." I stood up. "I'll be right back." Turning around, I hurried out the front door. After retrieving what I needed from the trunk of my car, I headed back inside. Then I held the hat out to London. When her smile faded, I realized what she must be thinking. "Okay, before you say anything, this was not the hat Calista was wearing. I've never let anyone wear this hat."

"What makes it so special?" She asked, sitting up and adjusting the pillow behind her back.

"It was my first Tigers' hat. The one they gave me when I made the JV team Freshman year. And I want you to wear it to my game on Monday."

A pensive look crossed her face. "How many girls have worn one of your hats to your games?"

148

Her question cut to my heart. *Damn Calista.* I never should've let her wear my hat. If I hadn't, then London would be first. And she should be first. "Only Calista, and that was a mistake."

"Why'd you let her have it then?"

"I didn't offer it to her. She sorta took it off my head and put it on. I should've taken it back, but I didn't have the heart to, I guess."

London stared at me a minute as if trying to figure out if she should trust me. I held my breath, waiting for her to respond. "Okay," she finally said. "I'll wear it."

When her fingers closed around the bill, I exhaled with relief. I couldn't wait to see her wearing it at my game on Monday.

It was the best game I played all season. My pitches were moving, and I was throwing gas. My team was all on their game too, and we won by six runs. It was especially satisfying because we were playing a team that we'd lost to in prior years.

If I had any question about my feelings for London, I didn't now. Seeing her in the stands wearing my hat made my day. Hell, it made my whole year. And I knew she was the reason I played so well. Knowing she was sitting in the bleachers cheering me on gave me the boost I needed. Normally when girls came to my games I found it kind of annoying. Sure, I liked the attention, but they always seemed to want something from me too. When I played baseball I gave all I had to the game, so I had nothing to give anyone else, let alone some chick I'd messed

149

around with. If anything, their presence messed with my mind, and I had to work that much harder to focus. With London it was different. Having her here made it easier to concentrate on the game. Her presence was a silent encouragement. It was affirmation. Never before had I cared what a girl thought about me, and it was crazy how much I valued London's opinion.

Honestly, everything was crazy about my feelings for London. They had taken me by surprise from the very first moment. This whole thing was insane – the way it sprung up out of nowhere and took over. The intensity behind my feelings for her were something I'd never experienced. I knew I should have been scared, but I wasn't.

"Hey, man." Nate slapped me on the back as we made our way over to the coach for our postgame huddle. "Great game."

"You too. That diving catch you made in the third inning was killer."

"Yeah, my arm is pretty scraped up, but it was worth it." Nate rubbed his forearm, and I saw the redness resembling a rug burn.

I chuckled, my gaze lifting to the bleachers. It looked like Grandma and Grandpa had already taken off, but London still sat in the same spot. She was bent over a device that looked like a tablet. It only took one second for me to realize it was probably her Kindle. My lips involuntarily twitched at the edges. That girl and her books. I'd never dated a bookworm before, and damn if I didn't find it sexy.

"You really like this one, huh?" Nate observed, his gaze following mine.

I nodded. "Yeah, I really do."

"Huh."

My eyes snapped to his. "What?"

"Nothing. I just never thought I'd see the day where Cooper Montgomery was whipped over some girl."

"I'm not whipped," I said.

"You should probably inform your face then. You look like a goddamn puppy dog around her. It's like she's yanking you around on a leash, man." He guffawed.

I narrowed my eyes. "You better watch it," I warned him, half joking, yet half serious.

He threw up his hands. "Hey, I'm just calling it like I see it."

"Did I ask for your opinion?"

Brandon jogged past. "Hey, great game, man."

"Thanks," I said. "You too."

"I'm only looking out for you," Nate lowered his voice as we neared Coach and the rest of the team. "Things are moving pretty fast with you and newspaper chick, and I don't want to see you get hurt."

"Don't worry about me, bro." I peered over my shoulder, my gaze finding London. "I know what I'm doing."

After the postgame huddle, I hurried over to London. She powered off her Kindle and slid it into her purse when I approached.

"Please tell me you weren't reading during the game." I climbed up several bleachers to meet her.

She smiled. "Nope. Surprisingly enough, I actually enjoyed watching the game."

"Watching the game or watching me?" I teased as I sat down next to her.

"Both," she responded coyly. "You were incredible out there."

"Thanks." I'd heard that from a lot of girls, but for some reason when the words came from her mouth it made my heart soar.

Several of my teammates were leaving the dugout, bags slung over their shoulders. A couple of them glanced over curiously, but I didn't care. I didn't care what anyone thought about London and me. Leaning forward, I ducked under the bill of the hat she was wearing and captured her lips in mine. "I love seeing you in my hat."

She smiled, catching her bottom lip in her teeth.

"You want to know why my hats mean so much to me?" I asked her.

She nodded.

I took my hat off and flipped it around. Then I pointed to the number on the back. "You asked me once if there was a significance to this number, and I sorta lied to you."

"Sort of, huh?" She cocked an eyebrow, her caramel colored eyes sparkling under the sunlight.

"Well, not sort of. I did lie to you." I took a deep breath. No one but my grandparents knew this, but it was important for London to know. "My dad was a great baseball player. He almost made it into the major leagues, but then he was injured. He's the reason I want to make it so bad; to make him proud,

152

I guess. Even though I know that sounds silly since he's not here." I shook my head, feeling like an idiot. London's hand found my leg. Her fingers caressed my skin through my pants, and I had to fight to keep my thoughts on the conversation at hand. "His number was eleven."

"That's so sweet." London smiled. "And for what it's worth, I think your dad is already proud of you."

Yeah, she was a keeper.

CHAPTER 19
London

Yawning, I stepped into the bathroom and shut the door. Once again I'd had trouble waking up even though I'd gone to sleep early last night. The truth was that I'd been too tired to read at night for the past week. Normally I read into the wee hours of the night and still got up in time for school in the morning. When I was a kid I used to hide under the covers with a flashlight, reading my latest book. Of course Dad would catch me every time and take away the flashlight. What he didn't know was that I could sometimes still see the words by the faint glow of the moonlight. I'd hold the book up to my bedroom window, squinting, as I continued to read.

Lately, though, I'd been exhausted. At first I thought it was because I wasn't sleeping well. The nightmares had returned with a vengeance a few months ago. I wasn't sure what triggered them all of the sudden. For months I'd been doing well, dreaming about my book characters. And then one day, bam, the nightmares about Mom were back. I didn't tell Dad. The last thing I wanted to do was worry him. He had enough on his plate. Besides, I didn't want to go back to see Garrett, my counselor. Not because I didn't like him. He was a nice enough guy, I just hated being analyzed. And mostly, I didn't like to talk about that day.

But ever since my date with Cooper on the bike trail I'd been worried that I was getting sick. It had been almost a week, and I wasn't feeling any better, or any worse for that matter. Every day I assumed something would change. Either I'd wake up with a spring in my step, or a frog in my throat. But neither had happened. I was still tired, still getting winded every time I attempted physical activity, but there'd been no cough, no fever, no throwing up. Honestly, it was a little disconcerting.

What was wrong with me?

Peeling off my pajamas, I discarded them on the floor and turned on the shower. It was hot, and steam rose from it circling my head and swirling up to the ceiling like plumes of smoke. Heat radiated off of it, warming my arm before I drew it back. When I did, a bruise caught my attention. It was on my forearm, large and dark purple. How had I gotten that? My stomach twisted, remembering a similar one on my calf. I didn't know how I'd gotten that one either. Swallowing hard, I dragged open the curtain and stepped inside the shower.

As the water cascaded over my body, I savored the warmth of it. I picked up the bar of soap, holding it tightly to keep it from slipping from my palm. Then I ran it along my skin, over the mysterious bruise on my arm, and along my pale flesh. The soap lathered, causing bubbles to rise along my skin.

Once I was clean, I rinsed my body and then turned off the faucet. When I opened the curtain, cold air hit my skin, and goosebumps appeared. I shivered as I stepped onto the bathmat and wrapped my body in a towel. After brushing my teeth and hair, I padded across the hall to my room and threw on a pair of jeans and a shirt. I was too tired to care what I wore, and I found myself dressing in an outfit I could only classify as BC (before Cooper). It wasn't until Cooper admitted he liked me that I actually began to care about what I wore. I still wore jeans every day. No matter how much I liked a boy, I wouldn't be caught dead in a dress or skirt. That so wasn't my style. But I had been wearing more stylish tops, and when I got a ride with Cooper or Skyler I wore sandals instead of my ratty tennis shoes. Today, however, I was riding my bike, so I supposed the t-shirt I'd thrown on would match my tennis shoes anyway.

Once I was dressed, I could hear Dad rummaging around in the kitchen. The scent of coffee reached my nose, and I inhaled. My eyelids lowered, my shoulders slumping. What I wouldn't give to crawl into bed and go back to sleep. Just the thought of riding my bike all the way to school was enough to cause weariness to sink into my bones. I wondered if maybe coffee would help. I'd never drank it, but I knew it helped to perk Dad right up. He would walk around like a zombie until he'd had his first cup. Sometimes he even joked about how coffee transformed him from a grouchy monster to a cheery human being. (In case you weren't already aware, my dad was pretty corny most of the time).

I trudged down the hallway and entered the kitchen. The bright lighting caused me to wince as I made my way over to the counter where the coffee pot sat.

"Good morning, pumpkin." Dad was standing over the counter holding a cup of coffee in one hand and a breakfast bar in the other.

"Hey," I mumbled, reaching into the nearest cupboard. My fingers located a mug, and my hand closed around it.

"You okay?" Dad asked.

"Fine. Just tired."

His shadow cast over me as he neared me. "You've been saying that for weeks. Are you sure you're all right?" Reaching over, his palm covered my forehead. "Your temperature feels normal." He stared at me as I set the cup down on the counter and reached for the coffee pot. "But you don't look so good."

"Gee thanks," I said, pouring some steaming hot coffee into my mug.

"I didn't mean it that way. It's just that you seem a little too pale or something."

"I'm fine." After picking up my mug, I brought it to my lips and took a sip. It was bitter, and I cringed, wanting to spit it out. But the sink was too far, so I forced it down. "God, that is nasty. How do you drink that every morning?"

Dad chuckled. "It's an acquired taste."

Shaking my head, I put the cup down on the counter.

"Why were you drinking it anyway? You've never wanted to drink it before."

"I told you. I'm tired. I was hoping it would wake me up." Sighing, I leaned my side against the counter.

"You've been sleeping a ton lately." Dad's

157

eyes crinkled in concern. "You know what? I think I'm going to take the day off and get you in to the doctor."

"Dad," I groaned. That's why I never should've talked to Dad about this. He always went overboard. For years I'd been complaining to him about how overbearing he was.

"You're due for a checkup anyway."

"I'm fine, Dad. It's probably just hormonal or something." I was hoping the use of the word 'hormonal' would get him off my back. My dad was pretty cool about most things, the one exception being 'women issues.' I thought he would burst a capillary when I first had my period. He had no idea what to do. It would have been hilarious if I hadn't been so freaked out too.

But nothing was deterring Dad today. "Humor me, okay?"

"But I can't miss school. I'll get behind."

"You haven't missed a day all year, and you have straight A's. I'm sure you'll be fine." He gently grabbed my shoulders and rotated me around. "Go lie down, and I'll call the doctor."

I wanted to protest again, but the idea of lying down was so tempting that I did as I was told. In minutes I fell into a deep sleep. I dreamt of blood, of Mom's eyes wide and filled with terror. And of a dark-haired man with black eyes and a fake smile. A smile I never would've trusted. So why had she?

Tossing and turning, I fisted the sheets in my hand. Even in my sleep I knew I was whimpering. The sound was faint, but I heard it off in the distance. Coiling the sheets around my fingers, I gripped so hard they cut off the circulation.

"London? Dad pried the sheet from my hand when he woke me up. "Shh, it's okay. It's Dad. You're all right. You're safe." It was the same thing he used to say when I was little and had nightmares. When my eyes popped open, I could see that all too familiar expression on his face. He knew. "How long have you been having them again?"

Pressing my lips together, I stayed silent.

"London, I can't help you if you don't tell me."

"Not long," I said. "It's no big deal." Swinging my legs out from under the covers, I slid them off the bed. "Let's get this doctor's appointment over with so I can get on with my life."

"All right." Dad stood, still appearing concerned. "I'll let it go for now, but only because it's time for your doctor's appointment."

"One thing at a time," I said, regurgitating a phrase Dad had used incessantly over the years.

"One thing at a time." He nodded, a small smile flickering.

Cooper had texted me several times while I'd been napping. I shot off a text on the way to the doctor's office to let him know what was going on. His response was one of concern, reminding me of Dad. I downplayed the entire thing, explaining that my dad was known for being overprotective. But the truth was that deep down I was a little worried too. I knew my body, and something was off. I'd been ignoring it for weeks, telling myself it was my overactive imagination and there was nothing to worry about. But somewhere deep inside me I knew that wasn't right.

Dr. Jeffrey's had been my pediatrician since we first moved to Folsom. He was an older gentlemen with bushy grey eyebrows and salt and pepper hair. He wore large black rimmed glasses, khaki pants, and a blue dress shirt, a stethoscope around his neck. His voice was soothing and, like when I was younger, I instantly relaxed as he examined me.

He asked the usual questions:

How long had I been feeling this way?

Did I have any other symptoms?

Had my diet changed?

My physical activity?

Was I taking drugs?

Having sex?

You know, the usual embarrassing questions doctors had to ask you when you were seventeen years old. Normally these questions didn't faze me, but this time when he asked the sex question my stomach did this little flip. Sex was not something I thought about very often. And when I did, it always involved my current book boyfriend, not a living breathing human. And I was pretty sure sex with a fictional character wasn't even possible. As real as they seemed to me, I was sane enough to know they weren't actually real.

But now I was dating Cooper, so my fantasies had suddenly traveled right out of the pages of my novels to a real live boy. And that both excited and terrified me at the same time. Still we hadn't had sex yet, so I told him that. I was glad Dad had decided to stay in the waiting room. Even though I had nothing to hide, I knew the sex question would freak him out. As cool as he was being about Cooper, I knew he was a little uncomfortable with me seeing someone.

"I'm going to send you to the lab for some blood tests, okay?" Dr. Jeffreys scrawled some words on a lab sheet and handed it to me. I couldn't read what it said.

Nodding, I dropped off the examination table, the bottom of my shoes hitting the linoleum. The paper quivered in between my fingers as I walked out of the room. When I got to the waiting room Dad stood, setting the magazine he'd been reading on the chair he'd vacated.

"What did he say?"

"To go to the lab for some blood tests."

"That's good, right? It means we'll know for sure what's going on." He smiled.

"Yeah." Still, I couldn't fight the nagging in the pit of my stomach as we made our way to the lab. After giving the receptionist my lab slip, I sat down next to Dad to wait. The room was full and I knew we'd be waiting awhile. While Dad picked up a magazine and started flipping through it, I yanked out my cell phone. There was a text from Skyler.

Skyler: Where r u? I'm sitting alone at lunch. It sucks.

Me: Sorry. I wasn't feeling well so Dad made me go to the doctor.

Skyler: What's wrong?

Me: Just tired.

Skyler: Maybe you have mono. It's all that kissing you're doing.

I giggled, and Dad glanced over at me. Smothering my phone with my hand I smiled innocently at him. He might have been okay with my relationship with Cooper, but I was sure he didn't want to hear about us kissing.

Skyler: It would be worth it though. I'd kiss Cooper even if I knew it would give me mono.

Me: Don't even think about it.

Skyler: lol

My phone rang in my palm, Cooper's number filling the screen. I pressed the talk button and brought it to my ear.

"Hey," I said.

A few people looked over curiously, and the receptionist gave me a dirty look. Dad raised his brow as if asking who it was.

I covered the phone with my palm and stood. "It's Cooper. I'll step outside. Come get me if they call my name."

Dad nodded before returning to his magazine article.

"Sorry about that. I'm stepping outside." The door dinged when I pressed it open. After stepping outside, I leaned against the large glass window on the building.

"Do they know what's wrong yet?"

"Not yet. I'm in the lab waiting on a blood test, but I'm sure I'm fine," I said. "Skyler thinks its mono."

"Mono?"

"Yeah because it makes you tired," I

162

explained.

"Ah, I see."

"Did you give me mono, Cooper?"

"Why would you assume you got it from me?" he asked. I could hear noises in the background, chatter and laughter, the sounds of the high school cafeteria. I'd rather be there than here.

"Because you get it from kissing," I lowered my voice, my cheeks flushing as a couple walked past. But they didn't even notice me. They were deep in conversation.

"That's herpes."

"You have herpes?" I joked, talking even lower than before and cupping my hand around my mouth so no one could hear. "I probably should have asked for your medical records before we started seeing each other."

"Ha, ha, very funny."

"Who's joking? I'm dead serious."

"Glad to see you still have your sense of humor. You must not be that sick." I could practically hear the relief in his voice. I pictured his dimpled smile and some of my earlier worry dissipated a bit.

"Yeah. Like I said, I'm sure I'm fine."

PART 2
AFTER

CHAPTER 20
London

It's funny how drastically life can change in an instant.

One minute I was a seventeen-year-old high school student, trying to get good grades and dating a boy for the first time. Then in the next minute I was being diagnosed with Myelodysplastic Syndrome. Now instead of worrying about whether or not I'd get into a good college after high school, I was worried I wouldn't live long enough to go to college.

I knew something was wrong when Dr. Jeffreys called within twenty-four hours of my initial appointment asking me to come back in. Usually I would get a call saying all my blood tests returned normal. I figured if he wanted to discuss the results in person, then it couldn't be good. But I had no idea he was going to send me to a clinic to have a bone marrow biopsy done. Honestly, I thought maybe he was going to tell me I had an infection. But never did the word 'cancer' register in my mind. Not until it fell from the doctor's lips. Even so, I stayed strong during the biopsy and in the days that followed while I waited for the results. I kept positive, certain they would find nothing. Perhaps I was severely anemic. That's what I kept telling myself. It's how I got through the days when the phone didn't ring, where no answers came.

Now I sort of wished I could go back to not knowing. They say that knowledge is power, but I was questioning that theory now. *Ignorance is bliss.* Now that's a phrase I could get behind. My mind flew back a few weeks ago to when Cooper was declaring his feelings for me. At the time I thought I had the world at my fingertips, that it was mine for the taking. I remembered the first time he walked me to my locker, how I had felt on top of the universe. Even when I was tired on our bike ride I wasn't worried. Nothing could damper my excitement at having my first kiss amidst the trees and ducks, overlooking the lake. I had no inkling that my life was on the brink of changing in a horrific way. No way did I think my tiredness was something this serious. At most it was an infection or a virus, I was sure of that. Kids my age didn't get cancer; they didn't die. We had our whole lives ahead of us.

Isn't that what we told ourselves? It's like how we didn't like to watch the news, why we turned our heads when we saw something too difficult to stomach. It was easier to believe it could never happen to us. Only now I knew. It could.

Not only that, but it had.

And now I had to face it.

Cooper had been texting all day, but I didn't text him back. I had no idea what to say. How could I tell the boy I just started dating that I had cancer? I was sure he'd dump me when I told him. Not that I would blame him. He was too young to deal with this kind of shit. Hell, I would walk away if I could. I'd turn my back on this damn disease and never think about it again. I'd run until my legs couldn't carry me any longer.

If only it were that easy. If only I could outrun this. But I knew it wasn't that simple.

I could see it on Dad's face, could read the defeat in his eyes. And it pained me. It killed me to see him so consumed with worry. He put up a good front, but I knew him too well. It had been the two of us for years. We'd been alone since I was five, and I could read him like a book. Right now the terror he felt was written across his face, it was scrawled in his eyes, painted in the lines of his flesh.

Not that I needed the confirmation. I had heard the bleak prognosis with my own two ears. The odds were stacked against me. The doctor assured me we could fight, but it wasn't a fight I was sure to win. If anything, winning would be kind of a miracle.

And I'd never been one to believe in miracles.

Stretching my legs out on my bed, I stared down at my phone as it buzzed. Now Cooper was calling. My stomach tightened, and I reached over and shut it off. I exhaled with relief when silence blanketed me. It's not like I could avoid him forever, but I needed a little more time. Time to gather my thoughts. Time to decide what to say and when. I thought about not telling him at all, but I knew that was impossible. First off, I had to start chemo soon, and I was pretty sure I wouldn't be able to hide the fact that I was losing my hair. Also, Dad wanted me to be home schooled the remainder of the year. As much as I hated high school, I felt like dropping out at this point was like admitting defeat.

167

"London?" Dad knocked on my bedroom door.

My head snapped up. "Yeah?"

"Can I come in?"

"Yeah."

The door opened a crack, Dad's head poking in. He looked tired, scared. Emotion rose in my throat, lodging in my tonsils and making it difficult to breathe. "Cooper's here."

It felt like someone slammed into my chest. Like Cooper threw a pitch and it knocked me right in the heart. "I don't know if I'm ready," I breathed, moisture gathering in my eyes.

Dad stepped into the room, running a hand over his head. "Honey, he's worried. I think you need to talk to him."

"I don't know how to say this, Dad." My lips quivered. "I'm not even sure I've processed it yet."

"Oh, pumpkin." Dad sat next to me on my bed, sadness swimming in his eyes. He placed his hand over mine. "I know this is hard, but you're a fighter. You always have been." Squeezing my hand, I could feel the desperation flowing through his fingers. "We're going to get through this."

I nodded, gathering up his words and wrapping them around me like a thick blanket.

"Cooper's been good for you," Dad continued. "You've been more alive since you started seeing him. Maybe he's what you need right now."

"I doubt he'll want to stay with me after he knows," I said.

"Perhaps he'll surprise you." He winked.

I sighed, knowing Dad wasn't going to let me

off the hook. "All right. I'll talk to him."

"Good girl." He released my hand and stood. "I'll send him back."

When Dad left, I scurried off my bed and raced over to the mirror above my dresser. I yanked a Kleenex out of the floral box sitting on top. Then I wiped away the traces of tears off my face. There was no way to erase the puffiness under my eyes or the redness on my nose, though. Hearing footsteps in the hallway, I swiped on some lip gloss and swiftly ran a brush through my tangled hair. Glancing in the mirror, I cringed. It wasn't much better, but it was the best I could do.

"Hey." Cooper stood in the doorway, hands shoved in the pockets of his jeans. He wore a navy shirt and a ball cap to match. Once again I was struck with how gorgeous his eyes were. For a moment I contemplated not telling him yet. Maybe I could put it off another day or two. Perhaps we could just make out tonight. That sounded so much more appealing.

But I knew I couldn't do that. I couldn't string this along any further. It wouldn't be good for either of us.

"Hey." I rested my elbow on the dresser in an effort to act nonchalant. But it slipped off, and I almost fell over.

"Whoa." Cooper stepped into the room and reached out to steady me with his hand. "Be careful there, Grace," he teased.

I giggled, the sound scratchy in my raw throat. But it felt good. After crying for the past several hours, a laugh felt incredible, freeing in some way. It loosened up some of the tightness in my chest.

His eyes met mine. "You gonna tell me why you're avoiding my calls?"

Way to get right to the point.

I bit my lip, and he circled my wrist with his fingers, tugging me forward. "Talk to me, London. I can handle whatever you're gonna say."

There was nothing but sincerity in his eyes, and I wanted to believe that what he said was true. "I have cancer," I blurted out, knowing if I didn't say it quickly I'd never say it at all. Knowing that if he kept touching me and staring at me with those bright blue eyes, I'd lose my nerve.

His head reeled back as if I slapped him, his fingers slipping from my wrist. He looked horrified, his mouth agape, his eyes as wide as baseballs. My stomach twisted. I knew he'd react like this, but it still hurt. He was staring at me as if I had leprosy or something. I was fairly certain he'd never touch me again, and already I missed it. Missed his hands on me, his lips covering mine. Anger burned through me at this horrible disease. *Why me? Why now?*

I'd already had a lifetime of disappointments, and when things finally started looking up for me this had to happen? *I swear, when I get to heaven God and me are going to have a real serious talk.*

"Cancer?" His words came out in a squeak, so unlike how he normally sounded.

I nodded. "Myelodysplastic Syndrome, actually." The look on his face told me that meant nothing to him, which I totally understood. I'd never heard of it before either. "It means that my bone marrow isn't functioning the way it should, and my

170

body isn't making enough normal blood cells."

"But it's treatable?"

I nodded.

"That's good, right?"

"Yeah, it is," I said softly, not bothering to go into what the treatments were.

To Cooper's credit, it didn't take long for him to smooth out his facial features. He took a deep breath, his gaze resting on my face. Reaching out, he touched my chin, his fingers sweeping over my flesh. This was it. The moment when he would end it. Since he was a nice guy, he'd do it in a tender way, no doubt. I swallowed hard, steeling myself for it.

"So what you're telling me is that it isn't my fault? I didn't give you some awful disease by kissing you?" He grinned.

I jerked my head up, shocked at his flippant words. Anger sparked for an instant before I realized what he was doing. He was making this normal, and in doing so he stole a piece of my heart.

Reaching for me, he grabbed both my hands. "So if I didn't give you mono or herpes, then would you please tell me why you're not answering my phone calls?"

"I thought…" my words trailed off, scared to say what I was thinking. It's not like I was out of the woods yet. He might still break it off with me. One joke didn't mean he was in this for the long haul. And seriously, how selfish would I have to be to want him to stay with me now? He was eighteen. This should have been the best time of his life. And the next few months were going to be tough. Did I really want to drag him into that?

"You thought what?" He drew me forward, his brow furrowing.

"Nothing." I shook my head, lowering my gaze.

Releasing one of my hands, he tucked his finger under my chin and pushed gently upward until I faced him. "Don't shut me out, London. Please. I want to help you."

"You do?"

"Yes, I do." Leaning forward, he kissed me gently on the lips. "Baby, I know this must be so hard for you, and I'm not going to stand here and tell you everything will be okay. People did that when my parents died, and it used to piss me off so bad. I won't ever offer you platitudes or empty words. But I'll be here for you. I'll hold you when you want to cry. I'll go with you to the doctor. Whatever you need."

It wasn't at all what I expected. We had only been dating a couple of weeks. There was no reason he should feel tied to me in any way. Staring into his eyes, I felt a mixture of gratitude and confusion. "Why would you do that for me?" I had to know.

There was that dimpled smile again. *God, it was cute.* "What kind of boyfriend would I be if I abandoned you when you needed me most?"

"B-boyfriend?" The air left me, and I swayed a little to the side.

Cooper circled his arms around my waist. "Yeah. That's what it's called, you know? When you're seeing someone and you really like them and you don't want them seeing anyone else. You're not seeing anyone else, are you, London?"

172

I shook my head.

"Do you want to see someone else?"

Again, I shook my head.

He lifted his hand, his fingers skimming my cheek. "Then I think that makes you my girlfriend."

Girlfriend. I caught the word in my hands and hid it in my heart. No one had ever wanted to be my boyfriend before. And I never thought when someone did it would be Cooper Montgomery. God, this was crazy. For a moment I forgot about the cancer, the bleak diagnosis, and the treatments. All I thought about was Cooper's words; about being his girlfriend. About the fact that he wanted to be with me, and only me.

And despite everything, I felt like the luckiest girl in the world.

CHAPTER 21

Cooper

I may have acted strong in front of London, but I didn't feel strong. Not one bit. When she told me she had cancer it was like someone had sucker punched me in the gut. I wanted to double over, to clutch my stomach, to hurl. But I couldn't do that. Not when she appeared so unsure, so small and frightened. She thought I'd bolt. I could see it in her eyes.

The truth was that I sort of wanted to. When the word 'cancer' slipped out of those cute little heart-shaped lips of hers, I wanted to turn around and run. Run with everything I had, and never look back. I mean, it wasn't like I'd been dating London that long. I had no obligation to her.

This was precisely the reason I never allowed myself to get close to anyone. I was scared of losing another person I cared about. Scared of having my heart ripped from my chest a second time. How many times could your heart be broken before it didn't work anymore? Before it was permanently destroyed?

But when I looked into London's eyes, I knew that walking away wasn't an option. We may have only been seeing each other for a couple of weeks, but I liked her a lot. And she needed me. What kind of an asshole walked away from someone like that? It was the same way I'd felt when she was lying on the side of the road wrapped around her bike. But this was worse. So much worse. And that made my decision even more crucial.

However, it didn't make it any easier. When I left London's house, a huge weight descended on my shoulders. I could hardly walk under the massive weight of it. My knees buckled, my shoulders tensed. I drove home with my teeth clenched, my hands white-knuckling the steering wheel. Even my music wasn't settling my nerves. Not that I was surprised. There was only one remedy for me tonight.

When I got home, my grandparents were on the couch watching TV. The canned laughter annoyed me as I hurried past the family room. After mumbling a hello, I told them I would be out in the backyard practicing. They didn't act as if it was anything out of the ordinary, and I suppose it wasn't. Even though it was late, I had been known to practice even later.

Storming outside, I headed toward my pitching net. After slipping my hand into my glove, I palmed a ball. Releasing all my pent-up anger and frustration, I threw it into the net. Again and again I threw balls into the net. The knot in my chest loosened a little bit, but it was still there.

So that's when I started yelling. A stream of expletives escaped from my mouth with each throw. My throat became raw, and my arm ached, but I kept throwing, and I kept yelling. I prayed that maybe when I was done I could leave this behind me. That I could be the strong guy London needed me to be.

"Cooper!" Grandpa's voice was like a clap of thunder from behind me.

I flinched. Dropping my arm, I sighed.

"What's going on, son?" His shadow cast over my shoulder.

Turning around, I took a deep breath. I had planned to lie, to say something about how I needed to practice. But when I looked into his eyes, it was like a well burst inside of me. I'd been spilling my guts to Grandpa for years, and I found myself sharing everything.

He didn't judge me or lie to me.

He simply placed his hand on my shoulder and said, "I'm sorry, Cooper."

"It's not fair." My earlier bravado withered, my body folding in on itself like an accordion.

"No, it's not," Grandpa agreed. "It's awful that London is going through this. That both of you are. If either of you need anything, you know your grandma and I are here. We'll do whatever it takes to help."

"Thanks," I told him.

"She's lucky to have you." Grandpa squeezed my shoulder. "I'm proud of you, son."

And, in that moment, I knew I'd get through this. I knew I'd be okay.

It was the first time London was meeting my grandparents, and she was nervous as hell. Frankly, I thought it was cute. I knew she had nothing to worry about. My grandparents already loved her and they hadn't even met her yet. But I'd talked about her nonstop for the past few weeks, so they knew all about her. Plus, they said that I'd changed since we got together. Said I'd softened or some shit like that. I wasn't sure why that was a good thing. It sounded suspiciously like what Nate had said about me being whipped.

"Do I look okay?" London shifted in the passenger seat of my car, tugging down on the bottom of her blue top.

Reaching over, I placed my hand on her thigh. "I already told you that you look gorgeous."

A broad smile swept her face, and it melted my heart. Damn, I'd do pretty much anything to see my girl smile.

Okay, so maybe Nate was right.

"I never told you this, but I sort of almost fell on your grandma at the first game of yours I went to." Embarrassment colored her words.

"Yeah, I know. I saw."

"You did?"

I winked. "You were distracting me even back then."

She chuckled.

"But don't worry. Grandma doesn't care. I told her that was you and all she said was that she thought you were pretty," I told her. "And she was right."

London nodded, clearly appeased.

We rode in silence for a few minutes, the radio playing lightly in the background.

"Do they know?" Her voice was barely above a whisper, and difficult to hear over the music, my tires rumbling, and the soft hum of the air conditioner.

But I did hear it, and I knew exactly what she

was asking. It twisted my stomach. The familiar anger that had plagued me since the first moment I found out about her illness rose inside of me. But I swallowed it down. I gripped the steering wheel so tight that my knuckles turned white. I'd promised myself I wouldn't lose it in front of London, and I planned to keep that promise. She spent so much of her damn time trying to make this okay for everyone. She worried about her dad all of the time. Hell, she even worried about Skyler. I wouldn't have her worrying about me too. "Yeah, baby." I squeezed her thigh gently. Already she was losing weight. Chemo wasn't starting for two more days, yet I feared she was already wasting away. It was part of the reason I insisted she come over for dinner. If anyone could fatten her up, it was Grandma. "They know."

She nodded. "I guess it makes sense that you would tell them."

"Did you not want me to?" I never thought about getting her permission before telling my grandparents.

"No, it's fine." Her face turned, and she stared out the window.

"What's wrong?"

She clasped and unclasped her hands in her lap. I'd always liked her hands. They were small and fragile, her fingers long and slender. But right now they looked too small. Everything about her seemed too small. How could someone so tiny fight such a huge disease? Fear clamped down like a vice, pressing on my chest.

"I don't want to be defined by this disease. I want to be London again. Not London, the girl with cancer." She choked on the words. "I don't want cancer to change who I am."

After flicking on the blinker, I turned the corner and my house came into view. "It doesn't. You're still the same girl you were before." Pulling up in front of my house, I parked along the curb. After cutting the engine, I turned to face London. Snatching up her hand, I took it in mine. "You're London Miller. You love to read books and make up stories. You have the most beautiful eyes I've ever seen, and your smile lights up your face. You're serious and quiet, yet incredibly loyal to those you love. You bite your lip when you're nervous, and it's sexy as hell. You're one hell of a kisser, and, best of all, you're my girlfriend." I winked. "Cancer can't take any of that away."

Tears glistened in her eyes. "You know what I think?"

"What?"

"I think that you're my savior."

"I'm not really a religious guy, but I've been to church before, and I'm pretty sure that's Jesus, babe."

"Not the savior of the world." She giggled. "I meant that you're *my* savior. You've been saving me from day one when you fought off the mean locker monsters."

I chuckled. "Never heard anyone describe Calista and her friends as monsters, but I'm diggin' it."

"And now you're still saving me." She blinked back the moisture in her eyes. "I don't know how I'd get through this without you. You're the only person that makes this bearable."

"Just bearable, huh? Then I'm not doing my job." I curved my hand around the back of her head and drew her lips to mine. Clamping my lips over hers, I kissed her firmly. Our lips brushed together, connecting and disconnecting with each subtle movement. The friction caused heat and passion, an incredible feeling unlike anything I've experienced. We were connected, London and I, fitting together like puzzle pieces. Our lips attaching as if they were made for the other. Her mouth was warm, her lips moist and soft. My tongue licked out, forcing her lips open. Clutching tightly to the back of her head, I massaged my fingers in her hair, and the silky strands tumbled over my hand. With my other hand I clutched her waist, my fingers slipping under her shirt and touching the bare skin of her stomach. As the kiss deepened, a small moan sounded in the back of her throat and her hands swept up my back. "It should be more than bearable," I said when we separated. "It should be mind-blowing."

"With you, it's always mind-blowing," she responded earnestly.

I rewarded her by capturing her lips with mine one last time before we got out of the car. As we walked up to the house, London glided on some lip gloss and smoothed out her unruly hair with her fingers. Before going inside, I reached over and helped to pat down a few of the tangled strands. It was my fault her hair was so messy, after all. Not that I would change a thing. Kissing London was pretty much my favorite pastime.

In the past, kissing was a precursor for what

180

would happen next. It was more of an appetizer before the big meal. But with London, kissing was the main course. It was savory and satisfying, and exactly what I wanted. Just like her. Wrapping an arm around her waist, I tugged her to me. She fit perfectly against my side, and it reminded me of how I'd curl up with my mom as a kid. A pang of sadness struck me, piercing my heart. My mom was the first woman I'd ever loved, and I'd lost her. It was why I'd distanced myself from real relationships. It's why I guarded my heart. Losing my parents was too hard. The hole their death left in my heart still hadn't healed. I wasn't sure if I could survive it again. And yet, I had thrown caution to the wind when I started seeing London. Now she was sick. It didn't seem fair. And it made me wonder why I was still pursuing this relationship when I knew it could leave me heartbroken.

London's fingers curled around the bottom of my shirt and she held tightly, clinging to me. Glancing over at her, she wore an anxious smile, and I knew why I wouldn't walk away from her. She needed me. And more than that, I needed her. I'd connected with her more than I'd ever connected with anyone else. Even if what we had didn't last forever, I knew I'd never regret the time I spent with her.

Smiling back at London, I turned the knob and we stepped inside the house. It smelled like garlic and spices, faintly of something sweet. My gaze swept the table, candles blazing in the center. Already there was a spread of side dishes and condiments. Grandma had gone all out like I knew she would. I'd

181

seen her poring through her recipe books a few days ago figuring out what she would prepare tonight. My grandparents were pretty up to date on the newest technology. They both had smart phones and Grandma had an ipad. But there were still some things they preferred to remain old fashioned about. Recipe books were one of those things.

"Hey, Cooper." Grandpa stood from the recliner he'd been seated in. "And you must be London." He outstretched his arm and shook her hand. "It's so nice to finally meet you."

"You too, Mr. Montgomery."

"Come in and make yourself comfortable. Dinner will be ready in a few." He swept his arm out, indicating the family room.

Before we could sit down, Grandma emerged from the kitchen carrying a large dish. She set it on the dining table and then looked up at us with a smile. Maneuvering around the table, she rushed over to London and pulled her into a hug. At first London was stiff, her arms pinned at her sides. But she quickly recovered, bringing her arms up and hugging Grandma back.

"We're so glad you could make it, London." Grandma drew back, grinning. "Any girl who can whip this boy into shape like you have is someone I have to meet."

There was that word again. God, was I really whipped?

When London's eyes met mine, I sighed. *Oh, hell.* She totally owned me, didn't she?

During dinner, London mostly picked at her food with her fork. She hadn't been very hungry lately. I wondered if it was the illness or nerves. I suspected it was both. Grandma and Grandpa stuck to benign topics, like London's hobbies. No one mentioned her illness or the fact that she wouldn't be returning to school this year, and for that I was grateful. She'd had her last day of school on Friday, and I know it was difficult for her. Even more difficult because no one knew why she was leaving. I could already hear the rumor mill chugging along. No doubt there would be endless theories making the rounds this week. London relaxed more with each minute. I could see it in the slope of her shoulders, in the way she gripped her fork. She spoke animatedly about the latest novel she was reading, and my heart pinched. I knew reading had always been her favorite form of entertainment, but it was clear that it took on an even more significant meaning now. It was her escape, her way of coping. I should be happy that she had something like that, but instead it upset me. She shouldn't have to escape. She shouldn't be going through this at all. Balling the napkin in my lap, I fought against the rage inside. *God, it was becoming a daily battle lately.*

The only awkward part of the conversation was when Grandma asked about London's parents. I had talked about London's dad, but I'd never told my grandparents that London's mom was gone. Maybe because I didn't know the whole story. I had no idea what had happened with her mom. It was something I'd wanted to ask her on more than one occasion, but she seemed to shut down every time the subject came up. I'd surmised that it wasn't something she was comfortable sharing. And I got

183

that. I'd been that way for years about my parents, skirting the subject every chance I got. Therefore, I respected her need to keep it private. I knew she'd tell me when she was ready.

Grandma appeared embarrassed when London had to share that she didn't have a mom around, and that it was just her and her dad.

But London made it okay by smiling and saying, "It's not so bad being raised by a man. Sure, I dress like a boy and I know more about fixing a car than I do about girly things like painting my nails or fixing my hair, but my dad's pretty cool. We make it work."

I reached for her hand under the table, wrapping my fingers around her cold ones. That's one of the main things I liked about London. Her ability to put people at ease. And to be honest, I loved that she wasn't a typical girly girl. I'd been with enough of those, and they weren't all they're cracked up to be.

After dinner Grandma poured some tea and brought out a pie she'd baked. London's face lit up as she bit into the flaky crust, strawberry sauce smearing her lips. Giggling, she wiped it away with a napkin and then dug in once again. She finished off almost the entire slice, and satisfaction sank into my gut. It was the most I'd seen her eat in over a week. Clearly she was a dessert girl. I filed the information away for later. I knew it would come in handy. Although, I had to admit the pie was amazing. I was still stuffed from dinner, yet I scarfed down my entire piece.

By the time we finished dessert, London's

eyelids lowered, and a yawn escaped. She threw her hand up to block it, but I still noticed it. Draping an arm over her shoulder, I leaned over and kissed her cheek.

"Ready to get home?"

I saw her wrestling with the decision. "I wish I could stay longer. I'm having such a good time."

"I know, baby." I rubbed her upper arm with my hand. "But you need your rest."

She nodded, annoyance glinting in her eyes. But it didn't offend me. I knew it wasn't directed toward me at all. She was angry with the disease the same way I was. It was one more thing that we had in common.

London pushed her chair back, and stood. "Thank you for everything."

"Of course," Grandma said. "It was great having you. You're welcome here anytime."

"Awesome. I'll be sure to come back next time you make that pie," London joked, causing both Grandma and Grandpa to chuckle.

After saying a round of goodbyes, I ushered London out of the house and into my car. It was dark and the air was cooling. London shivered as she settled into the passenger seat. I slid into the driver's seat and turned on the car. Light from the moon sliced across London's face, illuminating her pale skin.

"That wasn't so bad, was it?" I asked, guiding my car away from the curb.

"Not at all. I had fun."

"They loved you."

"I think they would've loved any girl you

brought home. They adore you, Coop." Sighing, she rested her head against the window.

"Did you call me Coop?"

She pressed her lips together, a guilty expression cloaking her face. "Oops, I'm sorry. I didn't even notice."

I hated when girls called me that. It was my baseball nickname, reserved for my buddies on the team. But hearing it out of her mouth was maybe the sexiest thing I'd ever heard.

"I liked it," I said.

She smiled. "How did I get so lucky?"

"Trust me, I'm the lucky one," I said. "And for the record, they wouldn't have loved any girl I brought home. They loved you, not because you were with me, but because you're you."

It killed me to go to school on Monday knowing London was heading to the hospital for her first round of chemotherapy. I would've given anything to go with her. To hold her hand when they injected the IV, to tell her jokes and make her laugh. I wasn't sure her dad would be able to do that for her. Not that he wasn't a funny guy. He was, in a corny kind of way. And he loved London in a way I never would. But still, he was hurting. Hurting like I could never understand. London was all he had, and she felt that every time they were together. She didn't verbalize it, but it was there in her subtle comments, in her demeanor. She was more scared of leaving her dad than she was of her own death. And I was afraid that would only make today that much more difficult

186

for her.

But London insisted I attend school. I had a game, and I wouldn't be able to play if I skipped out on school. Usually nothing could tear me away from the game. But today all I wanted was to be with my girl. Baseball didn't hold the same meaning when my girlfriend was fighting for her damn life.

Outrage filled me, and I slammed my locker shut with so much force it almost shattered in two.

"Whoa," Nate came up behind me. "What did that locker ever do to you?"

I wanted to chuckle and throw out some witty comeback. It was our thing, after all. But I couldn't. My mind was fixated on one thing, and one thing only – London. Blowing out a breath, I leaned my head against the hard metal.

"Uh-oh, what's going on?" Nate narrowed his eyes.

"I could take a guess." Calista swaggered in our direction, flanked by Lauren and Brooke.

I groaned. "Calista, go away. I'm so not in the mood for your shit today."

"I'm sure you're not," she answered seriously.

Now my curiosity was perked. *What the hell did she know?*

I shoved off the locker. "What does that mean?"

"C'mon, you don't have to play dumb with me. I know what's going on with nerdgirl."

I fisted my hands at my sides, feeling the vein in my head pulsate. If she wasn't a girl I'd pop her. But she was safe. I'd never hit a girl. Even one as evil as Calista. "Her name is London, and you'd be smart to start calling her that," I ground out the words between my teeth.

"Or I could start calling her 'your baby mama,' couldn't I?"

Her words confused me. "What the hell are you talking about?"

She crossed her arms over her chest, wearing a smug look. Her friends smiled by her side. Nate furrowed his brows in a look of confusion. At least I wasn't the only one. "I'm not stupid, Cooper. You're a manwhore. We all know that. And nerd---" she stopped. "I mean, London, isn't exactly experienced, so I'm sure she's not on the pill and doesn't carry around condoms."

I shook my head, knowing where she was going with this. My muscles buzzed under my flesh. "She's not pregnant, Calista."

She giggled. "Yeah, right. Who drops out two months into the school year? She's totally preggers."

I stuck my face in Calista's. "She is not, and you need to stop spreading these goddamn rumors."

"Really?" Calista raised her brows. A crowd was forming around us, and I needed to keep my cool. For London's sake. "Then why'd she drop out?"

"She didn't. She's doing home school," I said. All eyes were on me, everyone curious.

"Exactly. It's what you do when you're pregnant and trying to hide it." Calista grinned. "I guess I should start calling you daddy."

"Goddammit, Calista. What the hell is wrong

with you?" I spat. "Are you really that jealous that I picked her over you?"

Her eyes flashed, and I knew my words had hit their mark. I should have felt bad, but I didn't. This time she'd gone too far. My girl was having the worst day of her life and this bitch was spreading rumors about her.

"Are you kidding? Jealous?" Calista turned her nose up in disgust. "No way do I want to be barefoot and pregnant at seventeen." Snickers sounded around us. Whispered words swirled, the word 'pregnant' being the main one.

Shit. There was no way I could let people think London was pregnant. She didn't want people to know about her cancer, but wasn't this worse? Now they thought she was a slut who got knocked up. I slammed my hand into my locker so hard it stung.

Calista and her friends flinched.

Nate touched my back. "Calm down, man. Everything's going to be all right. I mean, it's not the worst thing."

Did he seriously believe what Calista said? "She's not pregnant, Nate." I craned my neck. "She's sick." Without looking at anyone, I pushed off my locker and stormed down the hallway. My intention was to go to my first period class, but I never made it. Instead, I found myself on the baseball field, staring out at the dark green grass, at the shimmering golden sand. My chest expanded as I took it all in.

"Hey," Nate's voice sounded over my shoulder.

I pivoted.

"How bad is it?" he asked.

I swallowed down the emotion that threatened to overtake me. There was no way I was losing my shit in front of Nate. "Bad."

"Sorry, man." Nate shifted uncomfortably on the balls of his feet.

"Me too."

"I think Calista feels bad too."

"I don't really give a shit what she thinks," I said.

"I get it." Nate nodded. "Is London going to be all right?"

I shook my head. "Not sure. She starts chemo today."

"Shit," Nate breathed.

"Yeah."

We stood in silence for a few minutes, both lost in our own thoughts. Besides, there was nothing Nate could say to make this better for me, and I was glad he didn't try.

CHAPTER 22
London

My hair started falling out.

When I woke up this morning there was a clump of hair on my pillow. The oncologist told me this would happen, but nothing could prepare me for when it did. I stared at the golden strands, taunting me from my pillow. I had been on chemo for three weeks now, and none of it had been a picnic. I was sick after every goddam treatment, I was tired, and I had lost my appetite. But this was by far the worst side effect. Reaching up, I touched my head, running my fingers through the hair that was left as a lump grew in my throat. I'd never been a vain person, but my hair had always been my favorite feature. Not only was it the shield I used to hide myself from the world, but it was my one feature I shared with my mom. Her hair was a little lighter in color, but it was the same thickness, the same length. In fact, I'd always worn my hair straight and long because it was how my mom wore hers.

And now I would lose it.

Angry, I snatched up the hair and tossed it on the ground. A growl erupted from the back of my throat, and I flung myself down on my bed. I knew I was throwing a tantrum like a child, but I didn't care. I was upset. I was hurt. But mostly, I was sad.

The squeak of the door opening sounded

behind me, and I stiffened.

"Hey."

I froze at the sound of Cooper's voice. I had forgotten it was Saturday, so I hadn't been expecting him so early.

"What's wrong?" My bed sloped downward, creaking as he sat down. His hand rested on my back.

Keeping my head pressed onto my bed, I pointed to the ground, to the strands of hair shimmering in the carpet. "It's my hair. It's-it's--" I choked on the words.

Cooper's hands swept up and down my back, creating warm friction. "It's going to be all right. You'll still be beautiful no matter what."

I shook my head. He meant well, but he didn't get it. I wasn't some shallow girl who was only worried about her looks. Hoisting myself up, I sat upright. Sniffing, I pushed the hair out of my face. "It's not about that." Lowering my gaze, I picked at a thread on my comforter. "I feel like I can't control anything about this damn disease. It keeps taking from me, and I'm powerless to stop it."

Cooper scooted forward until our knees touched. Snagging both my hands he gripped them tightly in his. "Then let's take control."

"How?"

"Hold on. I'll be right back." He stood up and glided out of the room. I heard him talking to Dad in the family room, but couldn't make out what they were saying. Then I heard footsteps in the hallway. Curious, I slid off my bed and padded over to my doorway, peeking out. The sound of a cupboard opening and closing came from the bathroom. When Cooper stepped out of the bathroom, he held Dad's shaver in his hand.

I reeled back. "What's that for?"

"I told you. We're taking control."

My body went hot. "Please tell me we're not shaving my head." Instinctually my hand flew to my hair.

Cooper's face softened. "You're going to lose it either way. You can watch it fall out a little at a time over the course of weeks or months. Or you can decide when it all goes."

I knew what he was trying to do, and I appreciated it, but I wasn't sure I could do it. Biting my lip, I stared into his eyes as if wishing the answer was inside.

"Tell you what." Cooper smiled. "I'll go first."

"What?"

He shrugged. "I'll shave my head first."

My gaze jerked up to his thick hair. "But I like your hair."

"Are you saying that you'll like me less when I shave it?"

I shook my head vehemently. "Of course not."

"C'mon." Tugging my hand, he guided me into the bathroom. Our bathroom was small and cramped. It hardly fit two people in it at one time. Cooper stood in front of the mirror, and I plunked down on the closed toilet seat. In one fluid movement, Cooper took off his shirt. I inhaled sharply, my eyes resting on the defined muscles of his chest, his pants hanging low on his hips and showing off the V like indentation. I'd seen his chest before. I'd even touched it, but I'd never get used to it. That I was certain of.

Cooper's lips tugged at the corners when he caught me staring. Blushing, I averted my gaze. What I wanted to do was leap up and touch him all over his bare skin, but I was acutely aware of Dad down the hallway, so I'd maintain some self-control.

After draping a towel around his shoulders, he turned on the shaver. It buzzed loudly in the quiet room. Standing up, I placed my arm over his. "You don't have to do this."

"I know." He smiled. "Trust me?"

Nodding, I pressed my lips together and sat back down. Hugging myself, I watched as he ran the shaver over his head. Clumps fell to the ground with each swipe. I winced as they crashed to the tile floor. Silence filled the room when he finished.

"What do you think?" He turned to me.

Standing, I ran my hand over his newly shorn head. The short strands were coarse and tickled my palm. I was used to burying my fingers in the thickness of it. "It's different."

"Good different or bad different?"

"Neither, I guess. Just different."

He stared into my eyes. "London, do you find me as attractive as before?"

"Definitely," I answered honestly. Short hair didn't change that much. He still had the same bright blue eyes, chiseled features, and strong jaw.

"Have your feelings for me changed at all since I shaved my head?"

I shook my head, knowing what he was

194

doing.

"And mine won't either." He stole a quick kiss on my lips. "With or without hair, it won't matter to me. I'll still find you incredibly sexy, and my feelings for you won't change at all."

My lips quivered. *How had I gotten so lucky?* "Thank you."

Cooper swallowed hard, his neck swelling with the effort. "Are you ready?"

I exhaled. "I'm not sure."

"You can't leave me hangin'." He nudged me in the stomach. "I was planning on us twinning."

"Twinning?" An involuntary chuckle arose in my throat.

"Yeah, isn't that what it's called?"

"Yeah, I've just never heard you say it." Cooper never ceased to amaze me. Glancing up at his head, I summoned up my courage. I couldn't believe he shaved his head like that. But he was right. If I did this myself, I couldn't say chemo took my hair from me. It would be my choice. My decision. I would be in control. And wasn't that what I wanted? Puffing out my chest, I stood tall. "All right. Let's be twinning."

"That's my girl." A broad smile swept over Cooper's face.

Breathing deeply in and out, I stood in front of the mirror. "But I'm not taking off my top."

"Man, that was the main reason I wanted to do this," Cooper joked, draping a towel over my shoulders. I fisted it, cinching it around me.

"Let's just get this over with."

My eyes closed when the shaver's loud buzz

195

filled the quiet space. I squeezed them shut with such force I worried I might pop a vein. The shaver skated over my head, prickling at my scalp, but I couldn't open my eyes. I didn't want to see the hair fall. It was bad enough knowing it was happening. I didn't want to witness it. Still, I felt it. I felt the strands as they slipped down my face, as they brushed my cheek, as they landed on my bare feet. Emotion swelled inside my chest, and tears rolled down my cheek. Each swipe caused more tears to fall.

"Oh, baby, it's okay," Cooper said, his hand stilling.

Flipping my eyes open, I gasped. *My hair*. It was really gone. A sob tore from my throat and tears streamed down my face, the salty taste lingering on my tongue. Cooper set the shaver down on the counter and swept me into his arms. I fastened my arms around his waist and pressed my cheek to his chest. Sobs racked my body as I cried into Cooper's skin, my tears wetting his flesh. He held me securely, his palms circling my back.

When I'd finally calmed down, Cooper framed my face with his hands. "You look beautiful, London. You really do."

Sniffling, I ran a hand across my nose. "You're just saying that."

"I never say things I don't mean. You know that." His thumbs wiped away my tears. "You have the most gorgeous eyes in the whole world, and now they look even more pronounced."

I wanted to believe him, but I wasn't sure I did. It was all too much. All I knew was that I needed to get out of the bathroom. I was starting to sweat, claustrophobia kicking in. And I didn't want to look at my reflection anymore. Blowing out a breath, I stepped into the hallway. As I did, I bumped right into Dad who had been walking toward his room.

His eyes widened when he got a good look at me, and it caused fresh tears to spring to my eyes.

"I'm sorry, Dad," I said, my voice wavering. "We- we- were trying to take control."

"Oh, pumpkin, you're beautiful." He drew me into a large embrace. "It shows off those incredible peepers of yours."

"That's what I said," Cooper interjected.

But he hadn't said 'peepers.' No one except my dad used the word 'peepers' anymore. But for some reason his use of the word gave me comfort. It felt familiar. When everything around me was changing, it was nice that some things could stay the same.

Christmas was hands down my favorite holiday. It wasn't so much the gifts, it was the entire season. It was magical, all the lights and decorations, the music, the feeling of joy and merriment. But nothing felt magical about this Christmas. When I woke up in the morning I felt groggy, weak, and sickly. Dad had Christmas music playing, and he was cooking bacon and eggs. He wore his Santa apron that I'd bought him years ago. I knew he was trying hard, so I vowed to make the most of it no matter how awful I felt. Besides, I was grateful to be home.

It was a hell of a lot better than being in the hospital like I had been for Thanksgiving. Dad and I had planned to spend Thanksgiving with Cooper and his family. It had always just been Dad and me for Thanksgiving. Some years we didn't even make a Turkey. It seemed that when we did make the entire meal, most went to waste anyway. Therefore, a cozy Thanksgiving at Cooper's house sounded perfect.

And it would've been. Only it never happened.

The week of Thanksgiving I acquired an infection and had to be hospitalized. So instead of an old fashioned Thanksgiving with Cooper and his family, I spent the day in a hospital bed, watching movies, reading books, and eating a few bites of hospital food.

As I sat down to Christmas breakfast with Dad, I was thankful to be in the comfort of my own home this holiday. Besides, I knew Cooper was coming over after he exchanged presents with his grandparents this morning, and I looked forward to seeing him.

I could only force down a few bites before queasiness took over. Dad must have sensed I was finished, because he wiped his mouth with a napkin and rubbed his palms together. "Ready to open presents?"

Following Dad into the family room, I dropped to my knees in front of the lit tree. Dad was bent over, his head hidden under the bottom branches. Pine needles brushed against his back, some of them sticking to his shirt.

Glancing up at the tree, my gaze swept over the array of mismatched ornaments. Decorating the tree was my favorite part of the holiday. Mostly because all the ornaments had been Mom's. It was like taking a trip down memory lane. Dad had a story to share for almost every single ornament. As my eyes lit on them, I recalled their stories.

"Here you go." Dad emerged, holding three small packages, a light dusting of pine needles in his hair and across his shoulders.

Sitting back, I ripped into the wrapping paper. After opening all three gifts, I leaned forward and kissed Dad on the cheek. "Thank you." I smiled, forcing down the disappointment. Dad had bought me a couple of novels I wanted and a leather journal to write in. I knew I wouldn't get my laptop. There was no way we could afford it now with all the hospital bills and Dad cutting back on his hours at the shop. Still, deep down I had hoped he could make it work.

To kill time until Cooper showed up, I decided to curl up on the couch with a cup of hot tea, a blanket, and one of the books Dad bought. It was called *Dazzle*, and it was the story of a group of warriors all with different special powers whose sole duty was to protect their town. It was funny because I could sort of see my relationship with Cooper played out in the story between the two main characters. The heroine and hero had gone to school together for years, but both had seriously misjudged the other. But the thing that made the biggest impact on me was the superpower of one of the sub-characters. Her name was Ariel, and she had the gift of healing. When I read that I paused, pressing the book to my chest. If only she was real. If only she could touch me with her healing hands, and make me better.

If only it were that simple.

But life wasn't a fairytale. Real life wasn't written in the pages of novels. It existed outside of the imagination of the author, and it couldn't be contained in three hundred pages, tying up nicely at the end in a happily ever after. Real life was messy with a bunch of loose ends like ratty cords all tangled up and disheveled. There were even some knots that were impossible to loosen, some strands that were cut and frayed. And we never knew how many pages we got. Some were given a saga, while others only a novella or short story. Worse yet, there didn't seem to be a rhyme or reason. Not like in books where the bad guy always got what he deserved while the good guys thrived. In real life it often felt like things happened opposite of that.

When I got about halfway through the book, there was a knock on the door. I knew it would be Cooper, but I still found my heart picking up speed. Dad raced into the room, leaving the kitchen where he'd been cooking dinner, and let Cooper in.

"There's my sexy bookworm," Cooper greeted me.

"I'm not sure about sexy." I reached up and touched my shorn hair. The day after Cooper had shaved my hair, Dad and I went to a beauty store and had a wig made. Right now it sat on my dresser. Usually I tried to wear it when Cooper came over, but the truth was, I hated it. It was itchy and I didn't look like myself when I wore it. The shop had done a good job with it, trying to make it look like my hair did. But to me it wasn't right. It wasn't me.

I missed my real hair. I missed the flush of my cheeks. I missed the little fat roll on my belly that I used to try every year to get rid of.

Quite simply, I missed me.

"Trust me, you're sexy. Hair or no hair." Cooper was always so blunt about everything. Sometimes it shocked me, but I was getting used to it. Plus, I liked how he never sugar coated anything. Dad treated me with kid gloves, like I was so fragile he was afraid the truth might break me. But Cooper didn't do that. Lowering down on the edge of the couch, Cooper sat near my feet.

"What's behind your back?" I asked, pointing to his hands that were securely hidden.

"So impatient," he joked, proffering his hands. In them he was holding several hats. "I know you don't like your wig, and I like seeing you in my hats, so I figure this is the perfect solution."

Sitting up, I grinned. I reached out, snatching one of the hats. "This one isn't yours. This is the A's."

"They're my favorite team," he said. "Put it on."

I nodded, and did as I was told.

"Perfect. I love seeing my girl wearing the hat for my favorite team. Now you just need a jersey."

"Why stop there?" I teased. "Don't I need a foam finger?"

He scrunched up his nose. "Nah, those are tacky."

I giggled as he set the other hats down over my legs. "They're all yours." Glancing up, his face grew serious. "But I meant what I said, you're beautiful no matter what. So only wear them if you want to."

"Deal," I said softly.

As if it was his way of thanking me, he leaned forward and pressed his lips to mine. It was a quick kiss since Dad was in the next room, and I found myself longing for more. It had been so long since we'd been alone.

Glancing down at the hats, I felt a pang of guilt. "I feel bad that I didn't get you anything for Christmas when you brought me such a great gift."

"Oh, this isn't your gift." Cooper smiled.

"It isn't?"

"Nope." He stood. "I'll be right back with that."

I was confused when he went back outside. Sitting up, I tried to see out the window, but I couldn't make anything out. When Cooper returned, he once again had something behind his back. Dad entered the room, wiping his hands on a dishtowel. The two of them locked eyes, both grinning. I looked between them, suspicious. What were they up to?

"Pumpkin," Dad spoke. "I know things have been tough financially for us, but I wanted to get you something special for Christmas. So Cooper and his grandparents and I all went in together to get you something."

My breath caught in my throat when Cooper swung his arm out from behind his back, revealing a box holding a brand new laptop.

"Oh, my god," I squealed, my hand slapping over my mouth. "I don't know what to say."

Cooper set the box in my lap. "I think that

202

smile said enough."

"Yes, it really did," Dad agreed.

As I looked from Dad to Cooper, then back down at my brand new laptop, my heart burst. I was learning that no matter how dark things became, with these two in my life, there was always beauty and light to be found.

CHAPTER 23
Cooper

At the end of January, London went into remission.

And I wanted to celebrate by doing something special for her. The holidays had been so awful for her this year. She deserved to have a little fun. So I took her on a trip to the snow. She told me the last time she'd been up to the snow was when she was ten. She and her dad had spent a weekend in Tahoe, making snowmen and having snowball fights. And she loved it, but they hadn't been back. Mostly because her dad was busy working, and they rarely took trips.

We weren't staying overnight, even though I wished we could. London may have been getting better, but her dad would never sign off on me taking her somewhere overnight. In fact, even if she was perfectly healthy and had never had cancer, I was certain her dad's answer would be the same. Dexter and I got along well, but he was still pretty protective of his little girl. Not that I blamed him. I was pretty damn protective of her too.

But it was okay. We had the whole day alone together, and that was enough for me. Since London had been sick, we'd rarely been alone. And I needed to be with my girl. I needed to feel her lips on mine, her hands on my body. I desired to touch her, to kiss her, to feel her body against mine. I wasn't used to staying this pure, let me tell you. I was the guy who hooked up with a new girl every week.

All London and I had done was kiss, and even that hadn't been happening very often lately. Not that I was complaining exactly. What I had with London was so much better than what I'd had in the past. Only for her could I be this patient. Besides, she'd been sick. How big of an ass would I have to have been to bring up the subject of sex with a girl who was ill?

But now she wasn't sick, and I was anxious to see where this day alone with her would lead.

She was wearing one of my Tigers' hats, a sweatshirt and jeans, but she had brought gloves and a knit hat. They were tucked away in her purse. Her eyes sparkled as I drove, and in them I could see hope that hadn't been present in the last few months. It was amazing the transformation that took place when she found out she was in remission. Sure, she'd been tough while battling the cancer. Tougher than I could even imagine. And she handled it better than I probably would have. But there was always this darkness in her eyes, like a light had gone out. It was nice to see that light back.

An hour into the drive we stopped at a little diner for lunch. After getting back on the road, it wasn't long before we started spotting snow.

"Look!" London pointed toward the shimmery white patches. Her face was flush, her lips curling upward at the edges.

Reaching over with my free hand, I laced our fingers together. "I have the perfect spot to stop at pretty soon. It has a little hill we can slide down and lots of open area to play around." I had a little sled tucked away in the trunk.

When we reached our destination, I popped the trunk to get the sled out while London leaned against the car and put on her hat and gloves. With her rosy cheeks and nose she resembled a doll.

"You are so damn beautiful," I said.

She giggled, and I couldn't wait any longer. Abandoning the sled in the trunk, I bridged the gap between us. Curling my hands around her waist, I tugged her forward. Her expression grew serious, her gaze dropping to my lips. I hooked my fingers into the belt loops on her jeans as her palms came up to rest on my chest. Angling my face, I lowered my head and crashed my lips into hers. There was no going gently this time. I couldn't restrain myself. She responded, her lips moving quickly over mine. Our tongues tangled together as she reached up, her glove-encased hands sliding up my chest, trailing over my shoulders, and resting at my neck. In my kiss I conveyed how grateful I was that she was better, how much I cared for her, and how much I missed this connection. As always, the kiss was intense; like an earthquake shaking the ground and splitting the earth beneath us.

"As tempted as I am to stand here all day and make out with you, I did promise you a day in the snow." Winking, I returned to the trunk and snatched the sled out. When I shoved the trunk closed, it slammed shut with a bang. "So, we better get to it."

Our feet crunched over the snow as we trekked across it. London shivered by my side, so I slung an arm over her shoulder. Sighing, she nestled into me. Damn, I was so close to tossing the sled and shoving her into the back of my car. Exploring the snow didn't sound nearly as exciting as exploring London.

But then I glanced over at her and saw her taking it all in. Her expression was one of awe. She loved it here, and I wouldn't take this experience away from her.

"What first?" I asked.

A stream of laughter filled the air as a few kids slid down the hill a few feet from us.

Her expression grew wary. "Um...I think I better start slow." Ducking out from under my arm, she bent down. Before I could register what was happening, a snowball hit me smack in the chest.

"What the--"

Another one hit me, and the sled slipped from my fingers. London laughed.

"Oh, no you don't." Leaning over, I scooped up a ball of snow. Standing up, I brought my arm back ready to strike. Then I caught sight of London and hesitated.

"Bock, bock, bock." She flapped her arms like a chicken.

I chuckled, lobbing a snowball in her direction. It landed near her feet.

"Seriously? Is that all you got?" She hurled another snowball toward me, but I sidestepped it and it crashed to the ground.

"London," I said, shaking my head.

Her shoulders sagged. "C'mon, Cooper. I know you can throw harder than that. You're not even trying."

"I don't want to hurt you."

She crossed her arms over her chest. "If you're not going to take this seriously, then why don't we just leave?"

"I am taking this seriously," I said.

"No, you're not. We came here to let loose, to have fun. Stop treating me like I'm going to break." Groaning, she stomped her feet in the snow. "God, I'm so tired of it! I want to have fun. What good is it to be healthy if everyone still treats me like I'm sick?"

Her words made me feel like shit. And I knew she was right. When she whirled away from me I picked up a snowball and hurled it at her back. It smacked her square between the shoulders. She froze, and slowly pivoted. On her face was a huge grin.

She bent down. "You better watch out, Mister." When the snowball left her hand, I lunged to the left and it barely grazed my elbow. Then I shot another one in her direction. This one got her in the leg, and she squealed. She tossed another one to me, but I caught it. Then I raced toward her, wrapping my arms around her middle and gently tackling her to the ground.

Giggling filled my ears as we landed. Her breath was warm against my skin as she breathed heavily. "Thank you, Coop." She kissed my lips. "This is the most fun I've had in a long time."

"It's not over yet."

"It better not be," she said. Then a shiver ran through her as her teeth began to chatter. "God, it's cold."

I smiled. "Does this mean you've already had enough of the snow?"

She drug her bottom lip through her teeth, and it took all my willpower not to bite it. "Nope. I think I'd like to try sledding. I've never done that."

"Sounds like a plan." Shoving off her, I stood. Then I held out my hand. She tucked hers in mine, and I yanked her up. "Let's go."

With her hand in mine, we walked over to retrieve the sled off the ground. Then we hiked up the little hill. It was one designed more for kids, so it was perfect. The last thing I wanted was for London to get hurt. As tough as she appeared, I'd never forgive myself if something happened to her.

"Last chance to back out," I said, when we reached the top.

"Coop, are you scared?" she teased. "You don't have to go with me, you know?"

I grabbed her around the middle. "That's it. We're doing this now." When I picked her tiny body up, she screamed. But it was a happy scream, not a frightened one. Tenderly, I set her down on the sled. Then I straddled her from behind, circling one arm around her waist. "Ready?"

She nodded, and I pushed off with my other hand. The sled began its descent down the hill. Icy wind whipped us in the face, and the ground bumped beneath us. London let out a little yelp when we crashed at the bottom. It wasn't bad. The sled fell over a little, and we landed softly in the snow.

After helping London up, she smiled at me. "I did it."

"You certainly did." I kissed her on the cheek.

"Can I do it again?"

"Of course."

After several more times London's lips turned blue. She shivered, her teeth chattering again. We were pretty wet from the snow by this point. "Wanna go back to the car and warm up?"

She nodded, still shivering. When we got back to the car, I turned on the heater and rubbed my palms together. London peeled off her wet sweatshirt. Underneath she only had on a white tank top. My heart stuttered in my chest.

"Can you hand me the other sweatshirt I brought?" She asked.

I glanced behind me to where her other sweatshirt sat in the backseat. I was tempted to tear off the shirt she had on, abandoning the other one in the backseat. But I fought against the instinct, and reached in the back for her sweatshirt.

As I handed her the shirt, I reached out and touched her bare skin. The pads of my fingers trailed up her arm and slipped under the edge of her tank top. Her skin was smooth and pale, ivory like the snow. She froze, her eyes on me. Leaning over, I kissed her shoulder, her flesh soft against my lips. Then I dragged my lips across her collarbone. Her sharp intake of breath was like a nod of encouragement. My lips skated up her neck, my tongue licking out at her skin. She arched her back, leaning her head back to expose her neck. As I peppered kisses all along her neck and collarbone, my hand slid under her shirt, running along her smooth stomach and up to her breasts. When my fingers inched under her bra, she stiffened.

"Cooper."

The stern way she said my name caused me to pause. I lowered my hand and drew back, confused. Without looking at me, she yanked the sweatshirt over her head and then hugged herself. It was like a slap in the face.

"Hey." I tucked my finger under her chin and guided her head in my direction. "What's going on?"

She sighed. "I don't know. I panicked, I guess." Her gaze lowered. "I'm sorry, Coop."

"It's all right. I never want to make you uncomfortable. I need to understand why. Is it me?"

"No." Her eyes snapped to mine, her hand touching my face. "God, no. I want to be with you so badly. I'm just scared, I guess."

"What are you scared of?"

"I don't know." Her eyes shot to the window, and my stomach dropped. There was something she wasn't telling me. Something big. No matter how much London opened up to me, I knew there was some part of her she kept guarded. A secret she wasn't ready to share. And I wanted to press it, to demand answers. But I couldn't. Not today. I wouldn't ruin this day for either of us.

I sat back in my seat, deciding to let it go for now.

A week after our trip to the snow, Grandma invited London over for a home-cooked Thanksgiving meal. It may have been February, but that didn't matter to Grandma. She'd find any excuse to cook and entertain, and London getting well was reason enough for her. Besides, she'd felt guilty ever since London had to miss out on Thanksgiving at our house. After seeing how much she loved pie, Grandma had been dying to make her another one.

London and I sat in the porch swing on the front porch. It was cool outside, but not cold. There was a light breeze, but the sky was blue, the sun warm in the sky. The scent of Turkey and fresh baked pie wafted through the walls, reaching us even out here. I swung us back and forth by pushing on the ground with the toe of my shoe, the chains rattling by my head. London's fingers were woven through mine.

"What are your plans now that you're better?" I asked her. "Thinking of returing to school?" Even when she was at her sickest, London kept up with her studies. But I knew she got bored sitting at home all the time. She'd confided in me several times that as much as she thought she hated high school all these years, she actually missed it.

"Oh, probably not." She shook her head. "Not this year. It would be too hard to go back. "Definitely next year though." Her gaze locked on mine. "Too bad you won't be there."

"I could stay. Do senior year again," I joked.

"Yeah, right." She giggled, resting her head on my shoulder. "But there is a writing class I could take at parks and rec. I've been thinking of joining it."

"You should. It would be good for you to get out of the house."

"You sound like my dad," she said.

Normally I had no desire to sound like a parent, but in this instance it didn't bother me. Dexter was right. Being cooped up in her house all day wasn't good for her. Now that she was healthy enough to get out, she needed to do it.

"Well, then I think you should listen to us." I nudged her.

"Oh, you do, huh?" She lifted her head, turning her neck in my direction. The sunlight spilled across her face, shining in her eyes.

"Yes, I do." I touched her cheek, my fingers sweeping over her smooth skin. "Have you been writing much on your laptop?"

She shook her head. "I want to. I'm just having trouble coming up with ideas."

"See. Maybe the class will help you." A car drove down the street, its engine upsetting the silence of the neighborhood.

"Yeah. Maybe." She nodded, but there was doubt in her eyes.

"What's stopping you?"

She hesitated, taking a breath. "I don't know."

"Yes, you do. Tell me."

"I've only been in remission a few weeks. I guess I want to make sure it's going to stick, you know? I'm afraid if I commit to something I'll get sick again and have to drop out."

"None of us knows what tomorrow will bring, but we can't live our life in fear." I ran my fingertips up her cheek. "Remember that day in the snow? How much fun we had?"

She smiled, nodding.

"That's how every day should be."

"Are you saying that you're going to take me to the snow every day?" She teased.

"I wish." I chuckled. "No, I'm saying that you need to approach life that way, and enjoy every minute."

"I know I enjoy every minute with you," she said.

"Me too." Leaning forward, I pressed my lips to her forehead, inhaling her sweet vanilla scent. And I silently prayed London would have an endless amount of minutes left on this earth.

CHAPTER 24
London

I knew it was too good to be true.

The past two months since I'd gone into remission were full of promise, hope and possibilities. But deep down, I'd had my doubts. Deep down, I worried that it wouldn't last forever. And that worry grew as it neared the time for my checkup and biopsy. The minute I saw my doctor's face when we showed up for my appointment today, I knew. He didn't even have to say the words. The results weren't good.

Dad was putting up a good front, but I could tell it was tearing him apart, which was why I didn't want to tell anyone else. Everyone had been so happy, and I hated to take that away from them. So when Skyler bounded outside the second we returned home from the appointment, I lied and told her it went well. And when Cooper texted, I told him the same thing.

Eventually I'd have to be honest, but I couldn't do it today. Give them some more time of ignorant bliss. I wished I could have it. But since I couldn't, I'd opt to escape in a different way. After talking to Skyler, I hid in my room with my latest novel. Curling up on my bed, I opened the pages and allowed myself to escape inside. Allowed my imagination to pull me into a world where there was no cancer, no illness, and no treatments.

"Hey." A voice startled me, yanking me from my fictional world. My door shoved open a little, and Cooper's head poked in.

"Hey." I was surprised to see him here. The spring season had started and he should have been at practice right now. "What are you doing here?"

"It's great to see you too." He walked to my bed and leaned down to kiss my forehead.

"That's not what I meant. It's just that I thought you had practice." I set the book down on my bed.

"I'm going there after this."

My eyes flickered over to the clock. "Aren't you going to be late?"

"It'll be fine." He lowered down beside me. Reaching out, he played with my fingers, stroking them gently. It felt good, and I longed for him to stay all afternoon and keep doing that. In fact, I could think of a lot of things I'd like to do with him. Perhaps if we did, I could get my mind off of the cancer for a little bit. But I couldn't let him miss practice.

"Coop, you have to go."

He threaded his fingers through mine. "I don't like leaving you."

"And I don't like when you leave."

"Then we're in agreement." He smiled.

"No, we're not," I said firmly. "You have to go to practice."

His gaze lowered, his eyes not meeting mine. *What was going on?*

216

"Coop?"

"A scout from Fallbrook University came to see me. He offered me a position on the team, and a scholarship."

I fought against the pang of regret. Truly I was happy for him, but I couldn't help feeling sad for me. I had no idea what I'd do without him here. But this was inevitable. He was a senior. And not just any senior. He was the freaking star pitcher of the varsity baseball team and a 4.0 student. "That's amazing. I'm so proud of you."

"I don't think I can take it."

My stomach tumbled to the ground. "Why not?"

His eyes slammed into mine. "I can't leave you, London."

"Yes, you can," I said. "And you have to. This is your future we're talking about."

"But I don't want to leave you." Dropping my hands, he stood. Running a hand through his hair, he grunted in frustration.

I couldn't let him throw away his future for me. This was what he'd worked so hard his entire life for. "I'm going to be fine. And lots of people have long-distance relationships. We'll make it work."

He swung around, his expression hard. "Don't do that. You know this isn't about us making a long-distance relationship work. And don't say you're going to be fine. Your dad told me what the oncologist said today."

So that's what this was about. My stomach clenched. Now it was my turn to look away.

"London?" His thumb tucked under my

chin. "Why didn't you tell me? You promised to be honest."

I stared out the window. The branches from the tree outside my window swayed, a blue bird flying past. What I wouldn't give to be that bird. To soar across the sky, untethered to the earth.

"Sorry," I mumbled. *Okay, so maybe I wasn't always completely honest with him.* In my defense, it was not an outright lie, just a lie of omission. "I didn't want to worry you."

"I get to choose whether or not to worry, okay? Don't keep information from me anymore." His tone was so firm it shocked me, and for some reason it sparked anger deep in my gut. It bubbled inside of me, my insides feeling as if they might explode like shaken soda.

"Okay. The cancer's back." I took a deep breath. "I'm sick again. It's worse than before and I might not make it this time. Is that what you want to hear?"

He fell to his knees next to me, grabbing my arm. "No, God, no. That's not what I want to hear at all."

Frustrated, I said, "Then what do you want from me? First you're mad because I don't tell you what the oncologist said, and now you're mad when I say it."

He dropped his head onto my arm. "I know. I'm sorry. I'm just so scared." His lips trailed my skin, his breath hot on my flesh. When he peered up at me, his face was ravaged with pain. "The thing is...that I think...no, I know." He paused. "I love you, London."

218

I sucked in a breath. He'd never said that to me before. In fact, no boy ever had. But I didn't have to think about it. I knew exactly how I felt about him. "I love you too, Coop."

"I don't want to lose you."

"I don't want to be lost," I whispered.

Lifting up on his knees, Cooper's hand slid up my neck. His lips brushed over mine, gently, softly. He took his time, rubbing his lips over mine, caressing every inch of my lips from the outer edges to the center. It was as if he was memorizing every ridge and nuance. His fingers trailed over the skin of my neck tickling the tender flesh. When his tongue slipped into my mouth I was ready for it. I tangled mine with his, creating a sensual dance. His lips sucked on mine, as his tongue swirled over my teeth and the roof of my mouth. It was as if he couldn't get enough. As if he wanted to feel and taste every detail. When we disconnected, I felt heady.

"You won't be lost," he said, framing my face with his hands. "I will always find you. I promise."

I nodded, knowing he was serious. The problem was I didn't understand what it meant. The simple act of loving me wasn't enough to heal my body, was it? It worked in my novels, but I didn't think it worked in real life. And as much as Cooper wanted me to live, I wasn't sure it was up to him. When my body was ready to shut down, there wasn't anything we could do to stop it. If the doctors couldn't stop the disease from progressing, what hope did the rest of us have?

On Saturday Cooper didn't have practice or pitching lessons, so we had all day together. Fortunately I was feeling a little better today too. Dad was out running errands. He acted like it was a spontaneous decision, but I knew he only went because Cooper was over. He rarely left my side these days. It was actually nice to not have him breathing down my neck. Not that I was complaining exactly. I knew he meant well, but sometimes it was a little overwhelming.

The air was cooling down, and it blew in through the open window, skating over my skin. I wore a pair of gym shorts, one of Cooper's Tigers' hats, and a jersey he loaned me. He kept telling me I looked sexy. I never tired of hearing him saying that.

"I've realized something." I threaded my fingers through Cooper's, sliding my thumb along his palm. "I don't have a bucket list."

"London." Cooper groaned, his grip on my hand tightening.

"No, hear me out." I knew he didn't like to talk about the possibility that I might die, but it was something I had to talk about. It was something I had to face. "I've read a lot of novels about people with cancer." I felt Cooper stiffen behind me, his chest hard against my back. "And all those books had this message about living your life to the fullest, and making the most of every moment. I haven't really done that. Most of my life I've hidden from the world." Releasing Cooper's hand, I turned to face him, sitting on my knees. "I don't want to live my life in fear anymore. I want to really live, you know?"

Cooper nodded, a pained expression on his

face. His hand came up to touch my chin. "You're going to have plenty of time to live."

My stomach dropped. "We don't know that."

His hand slid up, his palm curving around my face. "Yes, we do. You're going to live. You have to."

I bit my lip, my mind replaying the doctor's words over and over in my mind. My head lowered to stare at the hands in my lap.

"Hey." Cooper tenderly forced my face up to look at him. "No negative thoughts, okay?"

Nodding, I reached into my pocket and pulled out the folded up piece of binder paper. My fingers trembled as I unfolded it. The paper quivered in my hand.

"What's that?" Cooper raised a brow. His expression was a mixture of curiosity and wariness.

I took a deep breath, holding it out to him. "It's my bucket list."

He reeled back from it like it was a poisonous snake.

"Take it," I urged. "I want you to help me with it."

Hesitantly, he reached forward, his fingers closing around it. Leaning back, he scanned it. Then he sat forward and calmly ripped it to shreds. After throwing it on the ground, he stood. "No. We're not doing this," he ground out the words angrily.

Shocked, I found it difficult to draw breath. I stared at the remnants of my list, at the tattered chunks of paper littering the ground. *What the hell was wrong with him?* When I glanced back up, I saw that he was no longer in my room. Heart pounding, I slid off my bed and padded down the hallway. Cooper was flinging open the front door, sunlight spilling inside.

"Are you leaving?"

Without turning around, he shook his head. "I'm sorry. I can't do this." Taking a step forward, he slammed the door closed.

I flinched at the sound. Hugging myself, I stood in the hallway listening to the engine roar on his car as he turned it on. Slowly, I walked to the window and watched as he drove away. What did he mean when he said he couldn't do this? As I stared into the front yard, my gaze landed on my flowers. The ones I had planted a couple months ago. I had been so inward focused lately that I'd forgotten to water them. Now they were dying, their petals crunchy and brown, their stems bent toward the ground. They looked so sad and weepy, and for some reason the sight of this caused extreme sadness to blanket me.

My bottom lip began to shake, and a tear slid down my cheek. I wiped it away swiftly, but as soon as it was gone, another came, and then another. My knees softened, and I dropped into the nearest chair. I was like those flowers. Pretty soon my body would give out on me. I would no longer be vibrant and alive as I once was. And when that happened those around me would have to watch me shrivel and wither away.

I didn't blame Cooper for having second thoughts. It was too much of me to ask him to walk this journey with me. And I never should've sprung that list on him. What eighteen-year-old boy wants to spend their last summer before college caring for

222

a dying girl? It was selfish of me. If I really loved Cooper, I'd let him go. I'd allow him to enjoy his last days of his senior year, to prepare for his first year of college. I was done being selfish. If there was ever a time to grow up, it was now. It may have been the only time I had left.

CHAPTER 25

Cooper

I drove aimlessly around town. There was no destination in mind, but I needed to clear my mind. My thoughts were a jumbled mess, my stomach in knots. There was nothing I could do to make this sick feeling in my stomach go away. No way to stop hurting, to stop being angry. I felt like an ass for leaving London the way I did earlier. Ripping up her bucket list and running away was the wrong thing to do. I even knew it at the time. Still, I couldn't stop myself.

When I read that damn list, anger burned through me. Why did it have to be London? *Why her, goddammit?* She's the first person I'd given my heart to. The first person I'd allowed in, other than my grandparents, since my parents died. And I couldn't lose her.

God and I had never really been on speaking terms, but lately I'd found myself talking to him a lot. Begging him is more like it. Desperate pleas tumbled from my lips night and day. I'd even tried bargaining with him, offering to trade things for London's life. At this point I'd give up anything for her.

Pulling over, I exhaled and rested my head on the glass window. The sky above me was blue, sunshine spraying it. It seemed wrong that it could be so bright and cheery outside when it was dark and gloomy inside my heart. I was upset with myself for my behavior. My job wasn't to unload on London. She counted on me to be her comic relief, the one person she could feel relaxed around. She'd told me so herself. With her dad she often felt she had to walk on eggshells. That she had to be brave and strong for him. I had worked so hard to make sure she didn't have to be like that for me. But clearly I hadn't done that great of a job, especially if she had been keeping things from me.

And now I'd made everything worse by flying off the damn handle. God, I was such an ass.

The radio was on low, but the song playing was one I recognized. It was an older song, one my grandpa liked. I couldn't sit here and feel sorry for myself all day, but I wasn't quite ready to face London. Not until I got my head on straight. When I returned to her I needed to assure her that she could lean on me. That she could unload on me, and that I would be man enough to take it. I wasn't sure I was there yet.

But I knew who could help me get there.

Determined, I sat up straight and maneuvered my vehicle back onto the street. It was only a few blocks to my house, so I got there within minutes. Grandpa was outside tending to the yard as I had suspected he would be. When I got out of the car, I shoved the keys into the pocket of my jeans and trudged in his direction.

He turned to me with a smile, but it quickly faded as he took in my face. "Cooper, you okay?"

In that moment it was like everything came crashing down. London's illness, her dire prognosis,

225

her loss of hair and weight, the possibility that she might not make it. The stark reality that I could lose yet another person I love. All of it bore down on me until I could barely stand under the weight of it all. Slumping forward, I crumpled against my grandpa. His arms came around me, holding me firmly.

I wasn't the type of guy who cried. In fact, I couldn't remember the last time I did. It may have been when my parents passed away. Even when I broke my leg riding my bike I didn't cry. Sure I wanted to. I remembered pinching my eyes closed as tightly as possible, holding the tears inside. And when my lips quivered, I bit down on them. I was no sissy, I could tell you that.

But today I didn't want to bite down on my lip. I didn't want to keep the tears inside. I wanted to cry, damn it. I was tired of holding it in. It was time to release it, to let it out. If not, it would kill me.

So in Grandpa's arms I did just that. I allowed the tears to flow. And I held on to him, tighter than I ever had before. I clutched onto him as if my life depended on it. As if I was drowning in the sea and he was the raft sent to rescue me. And maybe that's what he was. I did feel like I was drowning, like the current was sucking me under and there was no one to yank me out. The fear and anger that consumed me was something I hadn't shared with anyone. It's not like I could tell London, so I'd kept it to myself, hidden deep in my heart. But in doing so, I'd made things worse. The waves were swelling, tossing me all around, and I'd done nothing to calm them. If anything, I'd provoked them.

I had no idea how long we stood there in the

middle of the front yard, my tears wetting Grandpa's shirt, his arms securely fastened around me. I was sure it appeared odd to the cars who drove past. Normally that kind of thing would concern me, but not today. Today it seemed petty, shallow, and insignificant.

By the time I finished, my throat was raw and scratchy, my eyes burning. Drawing back from Grandpa, I wiped my nose and face with my hands. Some of my tears had dried, and now my skin was sticky to the touch.

"I need to get back to London's." I sniffed.

Grandpa nodded. Then he reached out and gave my shoulder an encouraging squeeze.

"Thanks," I mumbled, as I stepped away from him.

"I'm always here for you. You know that."

And I did. His arms had been the same ones that held me after my parents had died. He'd lost his son, and yet he was able to comfort me, to be strong for me. Now I would do the same for London. I'd be strong even when I felt weak. And if I needed to unload, I'd come home.

To the people who had carried my burdens since I was a little boy.

And no matter, what I wouldn't allow London to give up. Instead I would stand by her side, and help her fight.

The shift in her behavior was apparent the minute she opened the door. In the hours since I'd last been here, she'd shut down on me. I could see it in her eyes. It was clear even in her stance, the way she stood with her arms crossed. It killed me. Not to mention the fact that she'd ditched my hat. It could've been that she got tired of wearing it, but it felt calculated. It felt personal.

"I'm sorry, baby," I murmured, wrapping my arms around her. She fell against me, but kept her arms pinned at her sides. "I got scared, but it won't happen again."

Bringing up her arms, she splayed her palms on my chest and pushed me back. Panic bloomed inside of me like a flower opening up. "No, you were right to get scared. And you were right to walk away. This is scary, and it's not your problem. You shouldn't have to deal with this. I get it."

The panic grew, unfurling. "You're right. It's not my problem." I took a step toward her. "You're not a *problem* at all, London. You're the girl I love, and I'm not walking away from you. Not now. Not ever."

Pressing her lips together, she shook her head. "But you should. You should walk away and never look back."

"I can't." Reaching up, I grazed her cheek with my knuckles.

"But you need to." Her lips quivered. "You were right to get mad earlier. I never should've given you that list. I'm asking too much."

"No," I spoke firmly. "You're not. I was an ass earlier, okay? I guess I thought if I ripped up the list, if we never did the things on it, then you would live forever." Feeling like an idiot, I blew out a breath. "I know it's irrational, but I need to believe

228

that you're going to make it."

She moved away from me. "That's just it, Coop. I may not make it. I might die. In fact, at this point it's looking very likely that I will die from this disease. Don't you get that?"

"Don't say that." I lunged forward, framing her face with my hands. "Don't ever say that."

She sighed. "It's the truth."

"No, it's not." Leaning forward, I clamped my mouth over hers, my tongue slipping into her mouth. All the pent up fear and desperation poured out of me with every push and pull, every caress and touch. I half expected her to push me away, but she didn't. Better yet, she responded to me, her lips moving, her tongue sliding over mine. Moving her arms up, her hands skated along my waist, resting at my hips. When our lips detached, I dropped my forehead to hers. "I win, London. It's what I do. And we're going to fight until we win." Lifting my head, my eyes met hers. "We're going to beat this. Together."

Her head bobbed up and down slowly. Hope sprouted inside her wide eyes. It was nothing but a tiny seed, but it was there. I could detect it in her irises. There was a spark that wasn't present earlier. And that was enough for me. As long as she still had some fight left within her, then it wasn't hopeless.

I nudged her. "Let's grab a piece of paper and we'll make out another list, okay?" Leaning down, I stole a kiss on her cheek. "And I'll help you check off every item on it."

"It was a dumb idea anyway." Lowering down onto the couch, she shook her head. "I can't change the past. It's too late for that. If I wanted to live my life I should've done it earlier. Instead, I've spent all these years hiding and covering up, never taking a risk and being completely guided by fear."

I sat next to her, snatching up her hand and knotting our fingers together. "What are you scared of?"

"Death. It's the same thing I've always been scared of." Her gaze traveled across the room, landing on the picture of her mom. "I never worried about getting sick before now though. That was never a fear of mine. The thing I've always been afraid of is dying the way my mom did."

"How did she die?" I asked tenderly, stroking her fingers.

She closed her eyes, taking a deep breath. "I was five. It was a Saturday, and Dad had taken me with him to the store. I remember being so excited because he let me pick out my favorite cereal. It was Lucky Charms, and Mom never let me get them. I was glad that she wasn't with us." Opening her eyes, guilt painted her expression. "When we got home, Dad was opening up the trunk to get the groceries out. He told me to go inside to get Mom so she could help us bring them inside. I remember that her gardening tools were out, lying in the grass. It was weird because Mom was always good about putting them away. When I got to the front door it was slightly ajar. That was odd too, but at five years old I didn't really think much about it. Instead, I walked inside. And that's when I saw her. Her shirt was torn, her pants down around her ankles, and there was blood everywhere. But the thing I've never been able

230

to get out of my mind was her eyes. They were wide. Wider than I'd ever seen them." London peered at me, her gaze connecting to mine. "Even in death she looked terrified."

Bile rose in my throat, and I swallowed it down. God, it was so much worse than I ever thought it would be. No child should have to endure that. Now I understood her fear of others, why she was so skittish. And it made sense why her dad was so protective of her. "Oh, London. I'm so sorry."

She bit her lip. "They caught the guy who murdered her, and he confessed. Told the whole story like he was proud of it or something." Her eyelids fluttered, her gaze fixated on her feet. "He said she'd been outside gardening when he approached. She'd been wearing a tank top and little shorts." London let out a bitter laugh. "He made a point of saying that in his confession, like it made a difference. Like he thought her outfit somehow had something to do with him. The guy made up some lie about his car breaking down and not having a cell phone. Mom was kind, like always. She let him inside to use our phone. That's when he….when he…"

"Shhh." I squeezed her hand. "You don't have to keep going. I get it."

Gratitude swept over her face. "I never trusted any guy after that. Well, until I met you."

Drawing her close, I pressed my lips to her forehead. "I'll never hurt you, London."

"I know."

"Do you?"

"What?" She breathed out, her lips parted.

"That's why you got scared that day in the

snow, right?"

"Not because I was scared of you," she said, her tone desperate. "I guess I've just always viewed sex as this scary thing ever since my mom died. Knowing what the man did to her--" her voice broke off, her bottom lip trembling.

"Hey, what that guy did to your mom was awful and sick. But that wasn't sex. That was violence. When sex is with the right person it is a beautiful thing, and not scary at all." I paused, looking deep into her eyes. "But I'll wait until you can see it that way before we do it, okay?"

"Okay." She dropped her head on my chest, her breath fanning over my skin. It felt good to have London in my arms. I thought back to that first day on the baseball field, how London wore that long-sleeved shirt and I'd teased her about it. Damn, I was such a dick. If only I'd known what I do now.

The sound of the garage door opening caused London's head to jerk up. Out of the front window I could see Dexter's car pulling into the driveway. Sniffing, London sat up. Lifting her hand, she wiped under her eyes with her index finger, and then swiped her hand under nose. Clearly she was putting on her brave face. Tires rumbled in the garage.

After studying London to make sure she was all right, I patted her on the back. "I should go see if your dad needs any help. Will you be all right?"

She smiled. "I can survive a few minutes alone. I'm not that close to death."

I threw her a stern look. "Not funny."

"Sorry." She chuckled. "But seriously, I'm

232

tired of everyone treating me like I'm so damn fragile." Peeling herself from the couch, she stood. "In fact, I think I'll help Dad too."

I didn't bother to protest. If anything, I admired her determination. As she walked toward the kitchen, I stood and followed her. We had almost reached the kitchen when London's body suddenly went limp. Before I could react, she slumped to the ground, her head hitting the carpet, her arms falling to her sides. I leapt forward when her body started jerking manically, her eyelids twitching. Panic seized me, and I reeled back.

"Dexter!" I hollered. "Dexter!"

The door leading from the garage to the kitchen popped open, and Dexter's head poked into the room appearing terror stricken. "What?"

I struggled to catch my breath, to speak. London was still twitching and jerking around on the ground. Thank god there were no objects or furniture near her. "It's London. She's…I think she's having a seizure."

Dexter sprang into action, racing into the family room and falling to his knees beside her. "Call 911. Now!"

I nodded, hot and cold flashes ripping up my spine. My fingers were shaking so badly it was difficult to extract the phone from my pocket. Even when I got it out, it was a challenge to dial since my fingers were slick with sweat. Turning my back, I walked into the kitchen, unable to watch London's seizure any longer. It was too painful.

After giving all the information to the 911 operator, I returned to the family room. London's body was still, but she was out cold. Why wasn't she regaining consciousness?

"The ambulance is on its way," I said, my tone hollow.

Dexter peered up at me, defeat written in the lines of his face.

"Dexter, what's happening?" I stared down at London's stiff body, grateful when I detected the slight rise and fall of her chest.

"I don't know, son." His tone was resigned.

Oh hell, no. He couldn't give up now. London was going to make it. She had to.

CHAPTER 26
London

The doctor's words had been like a splash of iced cold water to my face. They woke me up in a harsh and unforgiving way.

A bone marrow transplant was my only chance of surviving this.

No other treatment would work.

Without a transplant, I would die.

Sitting in the hospital bed, I picked at the white sheet with my fingers, fear consuming every part of my being. The window to my right overlooked another hospital building. I missed the trees outside my bedroom window, the green grass, and the colorful flowers. Everything about this place screamed death; from its sterile scent to its white walls.

"Hey," Cooper's voice rang out in the room.

I craned my neck to see him standing in the doorway. It should be a sin to look that good in a place like this.

"Hey," I responded.

His brows furrowed as he came further into the room.. "What's wrong?" Grabbing the chair in the corner, he dragged it along the ground and set it next to my bed.

"Besides the fact that I had a seizure earlier today and now I'm in the hospital, not much," I said sarcastically.

"But look at you now. You're back to your old feisty self, so that's a good sign, right?"

I knew what he was trying to do. He was trying to cheer me up, to make me smile. And usually it worked. But not today.

He scooted forward. "Talk to me."

"I'm scared," I whispered.

Cooper's hands found mine, our fingers tangling together on top of the stiff sheets. "I know, baby."

"No, I'm really scared." My lips trembled, and a tear slid down my face. "I'm not ready to die, Coop. I'm only seventeen." The words were coming out garbled, sobs breaking in between them. My nose dripped, my cheeks wet. Cooper released my hands and reached up to brush away the tears with his thumbs. "I thought I had my whole life ahead of me. There are so many things I haven't done."

"And we'll do them." His thumb was soft and warm against my prickly, wet cheek.

"When?"

"When you get out of here."

"*If* I get out of here," I said sourly.

"You will." His hand was still on my face. It felt good, yet I missed when his fingers used to tangle in my hair.

Grabbing his hand, I lowered it into my lap and stared deeply into his eyes. I needed him to hear me, to grasp what I was saying. "Cooper." By using his full name, I knew I had his attention. "It's not looking promising for me. My only hope of living is to have a bone marrow transplant, and it has to be

236

soon."

"Did they find out if your dad was a match yet?"

I froze. "How did you know my dad was tested?"

Dad had insisted on being tested the minute I was diagnosed in case it ever came to this. However, the doctor didn't seem too optimistic about it. Parents are rarely matches. Siblings, however, are the best bet. Too bad I didn't have one.

"Um…" Cooper's gaze shot to our hands. He rolled my fingers around, scrutinizing them intently. "He told me about it."

I narrowed my eyes suspiciously. It seemed that Cooper and Dad talked a lot more often than I realized. "Well, it doesn't matter, because he's not a match."

"He's not?"

"Nope." Shaking my head, panic bloomed inside my chest. "So now my doctor will look through the donor registry and try to find me one." I didn't bother adding how dismal my chances of finding a match were.

A nurse whisked into the room, her pants whispering with each step. She was different from the one I'd had earlier. "Just need to check your vitals, hon."

"Um…that's fine. I'm going to step out for a minute." Cooper stood, stamping a kiss to my forehead. "I'll be back soon."

Puzzled, I watched his retreating back as he scurried from the room. Perhaps it was finally becoming too much for him. I couldn't even imagine how horrible it must have been for him to see me have a seizure. And now to see me lying in a hospital bed hooked up to IV's and monitors, knowing that I may not survive. That's some pretty heavy shit.

As I held out my arm so the nurse could check my pulse rate and blood pressure, I stared at my hands, remembering how it felt when Cooper threaded his fingers through mine. Remembering how soft and warm his skin was, how it heated me up from the inside out. Closing my eyes, I conjured up the memory of his lips on mine, and I realized something.

I realized that Dad was right. With Cooper I was more alive. I'd lived more in the past eight months than I had in the seventeen years before that.

And maybe that was enough.

After the nurse left, Dad came into the room. "How ya doing, pumpkin?" He took the chair that Cooper had vacated. When Cooper had sat in it, it had appeared normal sized, but with Dad's massive frame the chair now resembled a child sized one.

"I've been better," I said, but forced a smile for Dad's sake. I couldn't tell him what I'd told Cooper about being scared. Dad was scared enough for the both of us, and I didn't need to add to that.

"I'm sorry I wasn't a match." Dad's tone was tinged in sadness. He leaned forward, resting his elbows on his knees.

"Hey, it's not your fault." Sitting up, I adjusted the pillow behind my back. However, no amount of adjusting would make this bed comfortable. I'd slept on floors more plush than this.

"I know, but I wanted to be so badly."

"I know." Out in the hall was a flurry of desperate voices, beeping, footsteps clattering. It made my stomach clench. I longed for home, for my bed, for quiet. And I wondered if I'd ever see it again. When I pictured Dad all alone at our house, despair tugged at me. I remembered what he was like in the days following mom's death. How he walked around wearing a lost expression, a perpetual black cloud hanging over his head. It would be too cruel for one man to endure so much loss.

Then I thought about Cooper. About how I'd admitted that I loved him. About how much I'd leaned on him in the past few weeks. It wasn't right. He'd lost too much in life already as well. Why was I holding on to him when I knew I might leave him soon?

"Oh, I saw Cooper in the hall," Dad interrupted my thoughts. "He's heading out to take care of some stuff, but he'll be back soon."

It was time to do the right thing, to stop prolonging the inevitable. There was no way to make this easier for Dad. He was in it for the long haul no matter what. But I could do something about Cooper. It was only going downhill from here. Let him remember me when I could still function, when I could still laugh and joke, when I could still offer him something. "Dad, when Cooper comes back, I'd like you to keep him out of my room."

"What?" Dad's eyebrows knit together. "Why?"

Shrugging, I said, "I don't think I should see

239

him anymore."

"But he loves you, honey."

"I know. That's exactly why I need to end this. I'm only hurting him."

"That's not true," he said. "You're not *only* hurting him. You're also loving him and allowing him to love you. Pumpkin, love is a risk no matter what. Tomorrow isn't guaranteed to any of us, whether we're sick or not. Your mom wasn't sick when we left for the store that morning. Nothing was out of the ordinary at all." He reached for my hand. "My point is that we never could have known what would happen. And if I had known I would lose your mom that day, I wouldn't have loved her any less in the days leading up to it. Loving your mom has never been something I've regretted."

A lump made its way into my throat. Dad's eyes found mine, the rich brown eyes that had been watching over me my entire life. The eyes that had narrowed when I was bad, that had crinkled when I made him chuckle. The eyes that appeared concerned at times, and proud at others.

"London, I'm believing in a miracle for you. But I need you to know that if we don't find one...." His voice wavered and he paused, pressing his lips together. "If we don't find one, and I lose you I will still consider myself the luckiest man on earth because I had the privilege of loving two of the most amazing women in the world – you and your mom. And that's something I will never regret."

I sniffed, my fingers slick in dad's hand. I rolled his words around in my head, but I didn't need to think about them for very long. I knew he was right. Besides, Cooper was so persuasive, even if I tried to push him away he'd weasel his way back in. Not that I would have been able to stick to my guns for very long. I loved him too much to shut him out, no matter how noble my intentions.

Dad blinked back the moisture in his eyes. Smiling, he waggled his index finger at me. "And you can stop pretending in front of me, young lady. I can handle this. I'm not going to fall apart. I have some pretty wide shoulders. Let me carry this for you."

Feeling ashamed at how I'd been behaving, I reached for him. "Dad, you are the..." I choked on the words. "You've always..." My throat was so thick it was almost impossible to shove the words through. "You have been..."

He moved forward, slipping his arms around me. "I know, pumpkin." I pressed my cheek to his chest as he held me. His heart thumped beneath my skin while his hand rubbed my back. "I know."

CHAPTER 27
Cooper

When I returned, London was talking with her dad. I peeked into her room and saw the tears in her eyes, the tremble of her lower lip. Dexter had a similar expression. Ducking back into the hallway, I stood against the wall, giving them privacy. Frankly, it made me happy that she was actually opening up to her dad; that they were having a heart-to-heart. I knew it was something they both needed.

A doctor wearing a white lab coat walked with clipped strides past me. Two nurses pushed a man on a stretcher in the opposite direction. Across the hall, a couple stood talking with a doctor. Their faces were drawn and pale. The woman held her hand up to her mouth as if she was crying silently into her palm. My heart pinched.

I'd always hated hospitals, but I hated them even more now.

Bending one leg, I rested my head against the wall and shoved my hand into the pocket of my jeans. My fingers skimmed over the paper inside, and my heart skipped a beat. I didn't want to come back until I had everything in order. Until I could give this to London. Adrenaline pumped through me as I waited with anticipation. There was nothing I liked better than surprising my girl. I loved the way her face lit up, the way her mouth curved into a broad smile that transformed her entire face. Other girls I'd dated expected gifts. They were like spoiled children on Christmas morning, always wanting more, and never satisfied with what they had. But London was nothing like that. She met everything I gave her with the same level of enthusiasm.

And this was going to be the best gift yet.

Dexter appeared in the hallway. When he spotted me, he walked in my direction.

"How is she?" I asked.

"She's struggling today," he said, his eyes flitting over my body. "Did you get it?"

I nodded, patting my pocket.

"And?" He raised one brow.

Grinning, I yanked the paper out of my pocket. It crinkled as I opened it. When I flashed it in his direction, a broad smile swept his face.

"Awesome. She'll love it." Dexter said. "And she could use some cheering up."

"That's what I'm here for." I grinned.

Dexter's hand clamped down on my shoulder, his face screwing up almost like he was going to cry. "I know, and I can't thank you enough."

I coughed, fighting back the emotion lodging in my throat. Before I could respond, Dexter wrapped his arm around me and pulled me into a hug. It was awkward and one-armed, but I appreciated it. He smacked me in the back gently, cleared his throat, and then backed away.

"I'm gonna head in." I pointed toward London's room with my thumb. "That okay?"

Sniffing, Dexter wiped his nose and nodded. With one last glance at him, I slipped into the room.

London lie in the hospital bed, her face upturned, her eyes closed. The sheet came up to her chest, her arms wrapped around her middle as if she was hugging herself. She appeared so tiny and fragile in the bed. My heart squeezed. As I walked toward her, the paper in my hand trembled between my fingers. I plunked down into the seat next to London's bed, and it shoved back a little, the legs scraping on the floor.

London's eyes popped open, her neck craning in my direction. "Oh, hey." She smiled lazily.

"It's okay. If you're tired you can sleep for a little awhile," I encouraged her. "I'm not going anywhere." As much as I wanted to give her the gift, I didn't want her compromising her health.

"I was resting my eyes a minute, but I'm fine."

"You sure?"

She nodded, the movement causing her pillow to rustle. "I'd much rather spend time with you than sleep right now."

"Great, because I have something for you." I clutched tightly to the paper in my hand, my palms filling with moisture.

"More hats?" she teased.

"You wish." I scooted forward. "But no. I've given you all of mine. Besides, what I have today is a million times better than a hat." Lifting the paper, I extended my hand.

"What is it?" Her fingers closed around one of the edges.

"Take a look." I could hardly contain my excitement.

Her gaze connected with the paper, and her eyes narrowed, her brows furrowing. "Is this what I think it is?"

Swallowing hard, I nodded.

"But how? I mean, when?" She shook her head.

"After I found out you were sick, I asked your dad what I could do to help, and he said I could have my bone marrow tested. So I did. It was around the same time your dad was tested."

"And you're a match?" Her tone was one of awe. "How is that even possible?"

"Well…" I moved from the chair to sit on the edge of London's bed. "The thing is that I'm not a perfect match, but I'm close enough." After taking a deep breath, I continued, "Your doctor didn't find any other matches in the registry, and you need the surgery as soon as possible. So, it looks like I'm your man."

"In more ways than one."

I chuckled, reaching for her hand. "I told you we would beat this together."

A serious expression darkened her face. "But what about baseball?"

"There's only three games left in the season." I wove my fingers through hers. "Not that it matters. You're more important than baseball."

"Baseball means everything to you," London argued.

"Not anymore."

"Are you sure about this? I mean, it's not like you're donating blood."

"Don't worry about me. I'll be fine. The

bone marrow donation isn't very difficult. It's an outpatient procedure with a couple weeks of soreness. No big deal."

"So we're really going to do this?"

I nodded. "We're really going to do this."

"See, I told you," she said with a victorious smile. "You are my savior."

"Careful, you're going to give me a big head."

She giggled. "I think it's a little too late for that."

"Hey." I feigned offense.

"Just calling it like I see it." London giggled again, and it made my heart soar. It was the happiest I'd seen her in days. That tiny seed of hope had grown into a full-fledged flower.

Nervousness wasn't something I was used to.

I wasn't a nervous guy. Sometimes other guys got nervous before our games, but I never did. Anxious, maybe, but in a good way. It was more like an adrenaline rush, and it always helped me play better. I'd never understood when guys would say that they felt like their stomach was filled with butterflies.

Until now.

Arriving at the hospital for my bone marrow harvest procedure, I was nervous as hell. And now I knew what it felt like. Let me tell you, it wasn't a bunch of sweet, pretty butterflies in my stomach, it was a swarm of damn bumblebees. They were eating me alive.

246

Grandma placed a quieting hand on my arm as we checked in. "It's going to be fine," she spoke soothingly, the same way she did when I was sick. It usually calmed me, but today I wasn't sure anything could. If only I could see London, then maybe I would feel better.

I saw her for a little while last night. The past two weeks she went through intense conditioning to prepare her body for today, so she hadn't been feeling great, but she was in good spirits. She was hopeful. Still, I worried. What if the transplant didn't work? What if it made her worse? All the words the doctor spoke to us during our appointments in preparation for today flew through my mind. Every statement, every word jumbled together, tangling like a million threads of yarn. But the one phrase that stood out above all the rest was: I am not a perfect match.

It was this phrase that plagued me, haunted me, mocked me. It whispered to me all night long, making sleep impossible to catch. I tossed and turned, worry holding me in its grip. What if I was making a mistake?

But it's not like I had any choice. I may not have been a perfect match, but I was a match. And I was the only one.

I was London's only hope.

And, damn, hope looked good on her. It brought the color back to her pale cheeks. It brought the light back to her eyes. I prayed it wasn't misplaced. We were all desperate for a miracle.

Please let this be it.

After checking in, we sat down and waited to

be called back. The nerves weren't settling. I sat forward in my chair, struggling to take even breaths. My leg bounced up and down so violently it shook the chairs around me. My cell went off in my pocket, and I dug it out, my pulse spiking as I wondered if it was London. But it wasn't. It was Nate.

Nate: Break a leg, dude.

Me: U know better than that.

It was a phrase we never used before a game. It may have been nothing but a superstition, but I worried that if we said it, it would come true. Breaking your leg was not something you wanted to do as baseball player.

Nate: lol

Me: Thanks tho.

Nate: Any time, bro. Text me later to let me know what's up.

Me: I will.

I shoved the phone back into my pocket and then resumed my leg bouncing.

Grandpa's hand landed on my back as I leaned forward, resting my head in my hands. "We're proud of you, Cooper. And I know that if your dad was here, he'd be proud of you too."

My head snapped up, my eyes locking with Grandpa's.

"You've worked so hard on baseball, son, and you're the best ball player I know. Your dad would've been over the moon about that. But what you're doing today shows what kind of man you are in here." Grandpa pressed his palm to his heart. "If your parents can see you from heaven, I know their hearts are swelling with pride today."

I pressed my lips together, blinking back the tears that fought to come out. After swallowing hard a few times, I successfully avoided a meltdown. Sighing, I sat back in my chair.

"You're doing an amazing thing for London," Grandma said.

Thoughts of my parents vanished, replaced by the image of London - about how frail and sick she was. Everyone was pinning their hopes on me. It was a huge weight to carry.

"I hope it works," I muttered into my hands.

"That's in God's hands," Grandma said. "All you can do is your part."

I peered up at her. "What if it's not enough?"

"Oh, Cooper, it's always enough. You're giving her the best gift anyone can give her – another chance at life. That's huge."

Nodding, I swallowed hard. "I want her to live." Reaching up, I ran my fingers through my hair. "I want a guarantee."

Grandma smiled. "Don't we all? But there are no guarantees in this life. You know that."

And I did know that. I knew that better than anyone. After my parents died, I used to replay our last conversation over and over in my head. Only I would change it, alter certain sentences. Like sometimes I would beg them not to go, and they would acquiesce. Afterward I would feel sick, wishing that was how it really happened. If I had begged them to stay, would they have? I'd never know.

I couldn't save my parents, but with London I had a chance. It may not have been perfect, but it was a shot. And I had to take it.

It was like when we were down in the ninth inning and it seemed like the game was over, but I still played with all I had. I never gave up during the game, and I wouldn't now.

I wouldn't give up on London. Not even if she took her last breath.

Even then I'd fight for her.

"Cooper?" My head snapped up to Dexter. He stood in front of me wearing sweat pants, a wrinkled t-shirt. His hair was mussed, his eyes blood shot and tired.

I shot out of my chair. "Is she okay?"

"She's fine," he assured me. "I wanted to come to wish you luck."

My chest tightened. I threw a silent prayer to the heavens. *Please god, let this work.*

After saying hello to my grandparents he pulled me aside, asking if we could have a word in private. My stomach knotted with worry as we moved to a quiet corner. I leaned against the wall, staring into Dexter's eyes.

He wrung his hands, turning his skin red. "That first time I saw you in my house I wasn't sure about you, Cooper," he started, his words slow and deliberate as if he was choosing each one carefully. "You seemed like a nice guy, but I still worried, you know? I guess I never see London as a young woman. To me she's always my baby." His voice broke a little. I fought to keep my emotions in check. "But then you kept coming around, and I could tell you cared about her. What I'm trying to say is that I'm glad she met you. I'm glad you're a part of our lives." Moisture filled his eyes. "I don't know how to thank you enough."

"You don't have to thank me, Dexter. I'm doing this because I want to."

"I know, and that's why it means so much. To both me and London."

"London getting better is all I want. That's the only thanks I need."

Dexter nodded. "I hope you get your thank you."

"I've never wanted anything more," I said earnestly.

"Me too," he breathed the words out, and they sounded like a prayer.

CHAPTER 28
London

Nausea rolled over me.

I breathed in deeply through my nose and out through my mouth in an effort to quell it. This had been happening ever since the surgery. Even though I'd been wheeled out of recovery hours ago, the nausea continued with a vengeance. The nurse assured me it was from the anesthesia and it would go away. I seriously couldn't wait for that to happen.

Lying back on the hospital bed, I stared up at the television mounted to the wall. Dad had put it on some old black and white movie before he'd stepped out to get a bite to eat. I was glad that he did. He hadn't eaten all day. Instead, he'd been glued to my side. And during surgery he'd been too nervous to eat. But I understood. I'd been pretty damn nervous too.

I hadn't heard from Cooper, but Dad had checked on him so I knew he was doing well.

Seems like we'd both come through the surgery fine. According to the surgeon there had been no complications. Now I just had to wait. The doctors and nurses would monitor me closely for signs of engraftment, meaning that new blood-forming cells would start to grow. They would also be monitoring me for signs of grafting failure. But I couldn't even allow my mind to go there.

As badly as I wanted to live, the main reason I hoped it was successful was for Cooper's sake. I'd never seen someone as excited as he was when he gave me his results. He wanted this to work so badly. And he'd been willing to give up practice and conditioning time for it. That may not have seemed like a big deal to most people, but I knew it was for Cooper. He rarely went a day without working on his pitching arm.

However, deep in my heart doubts resided. Before the surgery I'd made the mistake of googling bone marrow transplants. There were stories of success, but also stories of kids my age and even younger dying despite receiving a transplant. And I worried that I would be like them. That I would become another statistic, another story you could google on the internet.

If I died now, I'd never go to college, I'd never become a reporter, I'd never write that novel. And worse yet, I'd have to leave my dad and Cooper. I'd never been one of those girls who dreamt of their wedding day, or fantasized about one day being a mom. In fact, when I envisioned my future I was always alone. I was hitting the streets in my power suit, interviewing people and sharing it with the world. But now I sort of wanted that. I wanted a family one day – a man who loved me unconditionally, and children I could love and care for the way Dad had done for me.

Tears pricked at the corner of my eyes. I blew out a breath as another wave of nausea crashed over me. Reaching over, I clicked off the TV, and my room was silent. Well, kind of silent. Noises still abounded in the hallway – shoes squeaking on linoleum, papers shuffling, machines beeping, wheels rolling on the ground, and people chattering. But in my room it was just me and my thoughts. Even though the door was open, the curtain to my right was dragged closed blocking me from the doorway.

Lying back on my pillow, I thought about my mom. Not the one lying in a pool of her own blood with terrified eyes, but the mom she was prior to that. In the years since her death, I rarely allowed myself to think of her. Mostly because it was impossible to think about her without remembering the way she appeared when she was dead. That image of her was burned into my brain, branding me. Dad regretted sending me inside first, but how could he have known. I didn't blame him, but I did wish I hadn't seen her like that. I wished my last memory of her had been from earlier in that day, when she'd kissed me goodbye before Dad and I went to the store. The way she smelled like vanilla, the way her pink lips had stamped a lipstick stain to my cheek. The way she'd wiped it away gently and laughed.

I wanted to only remember the woman who had danced with me in the kitchen while she cooked, who tucked me in at night and read me stories. Mom liked to do all the voices. She was definitely the most animated storyteller I'd ever known. After she died, I never read any of the stories she'd read to me. I'd thrown all the books away. When Dad found them in the trash, he fished them out and attempted to read them to me, trying to emulate her voices. But it wasn't the same, and that made it even more painful. I ended up bursting into tears and cried myself to sleep that night.

The following day I saw them back in the trash, and we never spoke of it again.

In the months after her death, I longed for her in a way that made it hard to draw breath. But as the months turned into years, Dad was able to fill the void. Now I rarely wished for her. Dad gave me what I needed for the most part.

But right now I wanted my mom.

I wanted her to hold me. I wanted her to tell me everything would be all right, that if I never got to be a wife and mom that my life would still have meaning. I wanted her to stroke my head and kiss my cheek. In her arms I thought that maybe I would believe I could survive anything. Even dying.

With tears in my eyes, I whispered into the quiet room, "Mom, can you hear me? I like to think that maybe you're somewhere out there, watching over me. My own guardian angel perhaps." I smiled. "Maybe you're the one who sent Cooper to me. If so, thank you. I don't know how I would've gotten through any of this without him. And now it seems he may have saved my life." I swallowed the lump in my throat. "I miss you, Mom. I miss you every day. And I need you. Now more than ever." I paused, glancing around the empty room. "If I don't make it, I like to think that maybe I'll end up where you are. That maybe we'll finally have a chance to be together. Maybe then dying won't be so bad." Footsteps sounded in the hallway. Clamping my mouth shut, I listened. When no one entered the room, I continued, "But I don't think I'm ready, Mom. Don't get me wrong. I want to see you, but maybe not just

255

yet. Dad needs me. And I like it here. I'm in love. I'm happy. Anyway, if you have any pull with the man upstairs, I'd like you to ask him to give me more time here."

"Pumpkin?" Dad's voice sounded from the other side of the curtain. He dragged it open a little bit, and it rattled on the pole. When his face came into view he wore a mask over his mouth, similar to the one the surgeon had worn. Apparently all my visitors and nurses had to wear them since I was so susceptible to infection. "There's someone here to see you."

My heart skipped a beat and I sat up, wiping the traces of tears from my face.

"You all right?" Dad asked, taking in my face. His voice was muffled behind the mask.

"Fine." I nodded.

His gaze scoured the room. "Were you talking to someone?"

"Nope." I shook my head.

"Hey, girl." Skyler peeked around the curtain wearing the same kind of mask. It was blue, and it covered her mouth, held in place by strings that looped around her ears.

I was momentarily bummed that it wasn't Cooper, but that quickly faded to happiness at seeing my friend. "Hey, Sky."

Dad bowed out into the hallway while Skyler stepped into the room, hugging herself, her gaze shifting uncomfortably. She stayed close to the curtain as if she was being held in place by an invisible rope.

"I'm not going to bite," I teased.

Her face relaxed a little at my statement, and she walked in further. Still she kept her distance. The nurses probably had told her too, so I didn't push it. "How are you?" She spoke in a slightly muffled voice, and it was weird that I couldn't see her mouth moving. Just the rustle of the paper mask where her lips would be.

"I sorta feel like I was hit by a truck."

"That's better than a bus." She plopped down into a nearby chair.

"True." I glanced up at the clear liquid bag attached to my IV. "Maybe this is pain meds they're feeding me."

"If it is, let's hope they keep 'em coming."

"Right?" Another wave of nausea hit me, and I closed my eyes warding it off.

"You okay?"

I nodded. When it faded, I opened my eyes again. "Felt sick for a minute."

"You need me to get a nurse?" Her eyes flitted to the doorway.

"Nah, it's just the effects of the anesthesia. I'll be fine."

She sat back in her chair, throwing a strand of her dark hair over her shoulder. "It's super boring at home without you."

My lips tugged at the edges. "Your brothers still driving you nuts?"

"Always." She studied my face. "It'll be better when you come home."

"I'll be home soon, Sky."

She nodded, her eyes betraying the emotion she felt. Blinking, she sighed. "So, how romantic is it that Cooper gave you his bone marrow? I mean, it's like something out of a freaking movie. Bella and Edward have nothing on you two now."

I giggled. "I'm glad you're here, Sky."

"I'm glad you're here too, London."

Now the trick was going to be staying here.

"I can see my bone marrow is already working," Cooper said when he entered my room the day after the surgery, wearing his own mask. I longed to see his lips, to take in his whole face.

"What are you talking about?" I asked softly, careful not to wake up Dad who was sound asleep in the chair by my bed.

His eyes lifted to the television where a baseball game was playing. Giggling, I shook my head. Reaching down, I powered off my Kindle and set it on the table next to my bed. "Dad was watching it before he fell asleep. I was reading."

He came to stand over my bed, and I noticed he was moving slowly. There was a slight limp to his gait. "I thought maybe you were becoming more like me now."

"I don't think it works like that. They harvested your bone marrow, not your brain."

"Thank god. I would not want you having a peek in here." He pointed to the top of his head.

"Really?" I raised a brow. "Why not? Do you have something to hide, Coop?"

He glanced over at Dad. Then he bent down a little and whispered, "Just the thoughts I have about you. Not all of them are G rated."

I shivered. "Oh, yeah?"

"Yeah." He nodded. "And most of them involve you wearing this hat, right here." He pointed to the Tigers' hat that sat on the table near my bed. Even though I probably wouldn't wear it in the hospital, I liked having it close. It reminded me of Cooper, so even when he wasn't here, a part of him was with me.

"This hat, huh?" I glanced over at it, smiling.

"Yep, and that's it."

My cheeks colored.

"But don't worry." He eyed my dad, speaking in a low voice. "I'm a patient guy. We'll wait until you're ready."

Now it was my turn to glance over at Dad. I couldn't see his mouth behind the mask, but I could hear his deep breathing, and I imagined his mouth was hanging open. His arms dangled at his sides, and his eyes were closed. Thank god he was still asleep. There was no way I'd want him to overhear what Cooper had said.

I certainly wasn't ready for that, but I hoped that I would be one day. And if I was, I knew I'd want it to be with Cooper. He'd proven that he could be trusted. In fact, his body was a part of mine already.

Cooper dragged over a chair and plunked into it. "How ya feeling today?"

"Good. What about you? I couldn't help but notice you're moving kinda slow."

He nodded. "A little sore. Nothing I can't handle."

"Me too."

"That's because my girl is tough."

259

I smiled. "Sometimes. I have my moments when I feel like I might fall apart."

"But you don't. That's what's important. And if you ever do fall apart, I'll be here to catch you."

"I know you will."

"I love you, London."

"I love you too, Cooper."

EPILOGUE

Cooper

"This good?" I helped London sit down on the red plaid blanket I'd spread out in the grass.

"Perfect." She stretched out her legs, tilting her head toward the sky. She wasn't directly in the sun because I'd set our blanket in the shade, but it was still warm out here. By the expression on her face, it was clear she liked it.

I sank down beside her. It was the end of the summer, and London was recovering well. Engraftment had happened quickly for her, and her white blood count rose within the first month of the surgery. I teased her all the time, saying that clearly her body liked mine.

She would laugh, but I noticed she didn't deny it.

"Are you all packed?" London asked, running a hand over her head. Her hair had grown back a little. It was coming in thick and dark, not quite the same golden color as before, but close. She said she missed her old color, but I thought this suited her better. It made her eyes stand out even more.

"Almost." My heart ached when I thought of leaving for Fallbrook. It had been my dream to pitch for the Fallbrook Falcons for years. And a part of me

261

was excited. But mostly I was heartbroken over leaving London. In fact, I'd almost turned them down. But London talked me into waiting until we knew if the transplant worked. Once we found out that it had, she insisted that I go and pursue my dream. Still, I wasn't sure I could do it.

Ultimately it was Dexter who had talked me into leaving. He and I had become close since the surgery. We took turns caring for London, and because of this Dexter had been able to return to work at the auto shop a few days a week. When I told him how I planned to turn down the Fallbrook offer and stay here to attend junior college, he stopped me.

"If you truly love London, you'll go to Fallbrook."

His words surprised me. How would leaving London prove that I loved her?

"If you stay, London will feel guilty and you'll end up resenting her. Trust me, I know what I'm talking about. I've been around a lot longer than you, son."

At the time I'd argued with him, but he was insistent. A part of me wondered if it was his way of getting rid of me. London and I were pretty serious. Maybe that scared him. But deep down I knew that wasn't right. Dexter loved me like a son. Anyone could see that. Even my grandparents had commented on it.

As I mulled over Dexter's words, I knew he was correct. If I gave up my dream to stay here with London, she would feel guilty. Her selflessness was one of the things I loved most about her. And, the truth was that this was my one shot at possibly playing professionally one day. If I gave that up, it stood to reason that I would resent her at some point. As much as I loved London, I loved baseball too. And I owed it to both of us to see where it took me.

Besides, London planned to go to college too. Maybe not away. That hadn't been decided yet. But she still had a whole year to figure it out, to get stronger and healthier. I hated thinking of her finishing up her last year of Gold Rush High without me there to protect her. But she had Skyler, so I knew she'd be fine.

Speaking of which, Skyler's head appeared in the window next door. I swear that girl lived with her nose pressed against that glass. London and I both waved from where we sat in London's front yard before Skyler disappeared from sight.

"You better get packing, Coop," London said. "You're running of time."

"Any chance I can pack you away in my suitcase?" I nudged her in the leg.

"I don't think I'd fit," she bantered back.

"Oh, I think you would, Miss Skinny Minnie." I squeezed her slender leg.

She giggled. "That tickles."

"It does, huh?"

"Oh, no. Now I've only encouraged you." She scooted away from me slowly.

I gently tickled her leg, crawling nearer to her. She giggled as my fingers played with her tender flesh. But I knew I couldn't go much farther. Her body was still recovering. After I drew my hand back, she lowered her body down onto the blanket until

263

her back was flush against it. I stared down at her as she breathed, her chest rising and falling swiftly. God, I liked to watch her breathe. I loved seeing her alive and thriving. And I loved knowing that a part of me was in her body, that my cells were working their magic, healing her from the inside out.

Lying next to her, I wove our fingers together and stared up into the trees. Sunlight spilled through the leaves painting triangles of light on our legs. My toe touched hers. She wriggled it, displaying her pink polish. Damn, it was sexy.

Turning my head, I stole a kiss on her cheek. Swiveling her neck, she faced me. Her eyes sparkled in the sunlight, the flecks looking even more gold than usual.

"God, you're breathtaking," I told her, and her eyelashes fluttered. "I'm going to miss the hell out of you." Reaching up, my fingers lit on her soft skin.

"Me too."

"But I'll call and text every day."

"You better."

My fingers trailed her flesh, touching her chin, her cheek, then gliding over her lips. "I will. And you better promise to keep me up to date on your health."

"My body is healing, Coop." Her breath was hot against my fingers. "You don't have to worry so much."

"Promise me." *God, she was stubborn.*

"I promise."

Moving forward, our lips touched. A spark like static electricity shot through my body as our mouths connected. Her lips parted, eager, and our tongues melded together. My hand slid down her chin and skated down her neck. Warm fingers fanned my chest, tugged on the bottom of my shirt. When her hand slipped under the edge, I sucked in a breath. Her palm felt good as it slid up my bare chest, skimming over my muscles. Our mouths ground together, our teeth bumping. It was like we couldn't get enough. I growled and kissed her more firmly. A tiny moan at the back of her throat was her response. Her hand explored every inch of my chest, the pads of her fingers gliding over the muscles before curving around my shoulder.

"I love you, Cooper," she spoke against my mouth.

I tasted her words, savoring them. When I met London I hadn't been looking for love. In fact, I had been avoiding it, running from it even. I thought it was something I didn't want. But I had been wrong. Loving London was the best thing that had ever happened to me.

"I love you too." I kissed her again. "Always."

THE END
FOR THE GAME (Playing for Keeps #2) Coming Winter 2014!
Sign up for my newsletter to get release information, exclusive giveaways, and insider information: **http://eepurl.com/sp8Q9**

Author's Note and Acknowledgments

I've wanted to write a baseball romance for awhile. Mostly because I come from a baseball family. Pretty much every guy on both my mom's and dad's side has played baseball. Some even at a professional level, and many have coached into their adult years. But mostly I wanted to write this story for my brothers. Matt and Kagen are exceptional baseball players. Matt played third base all through high school and now coaches at the high school level. Kagen was a pitcher all through high school and is now playing professionally for a minor league team.

Both Matt and Kagen were my baseball experts as I wrote this book. Matt re-wrote most of the scenes out on the field so that they actually made sense. And all of Cooper's pitching jargon comes from Kagen.

The idea for the cancer portion of the story came later. At first I had planned to write this novel as a straight romance. The secrets of their parents' deaths were the only added twist when I began. But my daughter is obsessed with ugly cry books right now, and she's been begging me to write one. I already did with Cuts Run Deep, but she wanted one about illness. So I started outlining an idea for a story that involved a transplant. As I worked on that outline I realized that Cooper and London's story would actually fit it perfectly. So I revamped this story to fit that idea. And I think it worked really well.

I hope you think it did too.

As always I have a ton of people to thank:

Lisa Richardson, my super star editor. Without her you would read phrases like 'care feet' instead of 'bare feet.' I don't know what I'd do without her.

Kris at C & K Creations for my fabulous cover. I love it so much. It's perfect.

Cambria Hebert for being an awesome beta reader and catching all the crazy mistakes, and for helping me realize what needed to change for the second half of the book.

To Leanne Coulson for coming up with Fallbrook University. That was awesome!

To my kids for being so understanding when Cooper and London took over my life.

For my husband who is always super supportive and loves me so well.

To my extended family – there are too many to name but I love you all!

To all my readers, bloggers and fans, you make this all worth it! I can't thank you enough.

And, most of all, to God, who makes all this possible. Everything I do is for you.

Amber

Amber Garza is the au___   's *Gift Series*, the *Prowl Trilogy*, suspense novel _____d, and many contemporary romance titles, including *Star Struck* and *Tripping Me Up*. She has had a passion for the written word since she was a child making books out of notebook paper and staples. Her hobbies include reading and singing. Tea and wine are her drinks of choice (not necessarily in that order). She writes while blaring music, and talks about her characters like they're real people. She currently lives in California with her amazing husband, and two hilarious children who provide her with enough material to keep her writing for years.

18734703R00165

Made in the USA
San Bernardino, CA
26 January 2015